Jade

Tracey Chizoba Fletcher

Ukiyoto Publishing

For Grandma'am, Elder Mrs Mercy Ugenyi Ukpai, an unsung heroine of the Nigerian Civil War.

Contents

CHAPTER ONE

Gregory woke up with a start; the peal of the alarm still ringing on the nightstand. He groaned aloud as he groggily sat up. The early morning light had filtered in through the parted curtains. The clock flashed 6:00 a.m. but the brightness would have fooled him into thinking it was already 7:00 a.m. It was that time of the year where there were longer days and shorter nights.

Gregory shut off the alarm and trotted to the bathroom. Today was Monday, the first day of the new school year. He was now a senior secondary school student, having passed the Junior West African Examination Council Exams.

Thirty minutes later, he was out of the bathroom, a white towel draped around his waist. He stood in front of the body-mirror in his room, and pride swelled within him as he stared at his reflection. His chest had expanded; his shoulders had filled up and broadened, and his packs had began developing. He had been lifting weights during the long-term holidays. He could already visualise the stares from his mates at school: adulation and admiration from the females, and a mixture of praise and envy from the males. Gregory couldn't wait to see it in the flesh. He reveled in his look once more, lips curling into a wild grin, revealing a dimple on the left side of his cheek. He owed it to a trait he possessed—the ability to stay focused and committed to whatever he set his mind to do. It hadn't been easy, but here he was.

Gregory quickly had a handle on his thoughts. He grabbed an antiperspirant deodorant and applied a generous amount to his hairy armpit—a symbol of a grown man. He put the deodorant back to the shelf, but paused at the sight of the Vaseline lotion. Repulsed at the idea of applying cream to his skin, he pushed it back just as he heard a knock at the door.

"Come in," Gregory called out.

His mother, Mrs Ngozi Agwu, walked in. Gregory caught her reflection in the mirror.

"Good morning, Mum," he greeted, whipping around.

"Good morning, my son. Did you sleep well?"

"Yes, Mum," he replied, observing the worried look on her face. "Is everything okay?"

She sat down on his bed and released a dejected sigh. "It's your grandmother. She's at it again."

'At it again' meant that Grandma—his maternal grandmother—had woken up today not remembering who she was. She was sixty-five-years old, and had been diagnosed three years ago with Alzheimer's. Alzheimer's disease! Two words he hated. Gregory refused calling the name out from the day his mother informed him of what the doctor had said. Calling it out would give it more life. Make it real. He wasn't ready to accept it yet.

It wasn't far gone, though. Most times, she remembered who and where she was. But on days like this, when all her memory was upturned and she was difficult to handle, it was painful. The family doctor had warned that it would get worse, so his mother had her moved to their house to live with them, so she could watch over and take care of her.

Gregory ambled to his mother and rubbed her back, trying to placate her. "It will be fine, okay."

His mother had a faraway look in her eyes. Some seconds passed before she responded. "Thank you, my son. I can't prepare breakfast for you today. Please, take care of yourself while I attend to your grandmother. There is a loaf of bread on the dining table."

"Go ahead, Mum. I will be fine," Gregory assured her. He knew how she felt. His shoulders dropped as she walked away. She never said a word about Grandma's health, but the things unsaid were evident in her eyes. It would certainly be a bad day for her.

Gregory cast his eyes around, searching. He needed to hurry. He couldn't be late for school on the first day. When his gaze landed on it, his eyes brightened. It was the symbol of his new status. His uniform: a white short-sleeved shirt with blue stripes, the trousers—a dark shade of blue, and his tie, neatly pressed, all arranged neatly on the hangers.

He set about dressing up quickly. Then he knotted his tie just the way his father had taught him. When he looked satisfied with it, he made his bed, picked up his school bag, and stepped out of the room. His father had already left for work in order to beat the early morning Lagos traffic.

In the kitchen, he fixed himself a quick meal: five slices of bread with margarine smeared on top, one boiled egg, and a cup of tea. He stared at the clock in the living room. It was 7:07 a.m. He had to be in school by 7:30 a.m.

Gregory rushed to his grandmother's room. He knocked gently.

"Come in," his mother said.

He made his way inside. Grandma was plopped on an armchair opposite her bed. His mother was trying to get her to go take a bath. Hot water had been poured out for her use.

"Leave me alone!" Grandma shouted as she slapped his mother's hand away. Then she turned to him, her eyes devoid of the usual look of acknowledgement. "Ehen, who are you? Have you come to help this woman whom I don't know? Let me tell you people eh, if you come closer to me, I will scream for help. You are both kidnappers."

Gregory's mum sent him an apologetic look. He smiled at her in understanding. There was no need for that. They were in this together. He motioned to her, informing her he was leaving.

"Go well, my son. Be a good boy, okay."

Gregory chuckled softly and exited the room. He picked up his school bag from a chair in the living room, and sauntered out of the house, past the gate, and onto the street. A shout from behind startled him.

"Gregory, my man, this your trouser na correct o!"

Gregory recognised the voice. He turned around, taking in the sight of his three best friends: Abiodun—the speaker, Chima, and Eze. He laughed joyfully as they moved forward from the side of the fence where they had stood, waiting for him to come out. "My guys!" he yelled. "We don become big boys o!"

They backslapped and threw high five's.

"Senior boys, we are!" Eze said as they walked together to school.

CHAPTER TWO

7:30 a.m. didn't happen. They chatted, laughed, and played around, shouting at the top of their voices. Their numbers increased as they ran into more of their classmates on the way. By the time they neared the school gate with a huge emblem, 'Crescent Secondary School' sprawled on an arc across the gate, it was 7:40 a.m. The morning assembly began at 7:45 a.m., so they had a few minutes to get in line.

Loud banters and laughter filled the school grounds, replicating the scene they had a while ago. The teachers already had on their serious, stoic looks.

Banke, the only girl permitted to be close to their circle, ran towards them. "Look at my knights in shining armours," she exclaimed, taking in their new look.

"We are perfect gentlemen," Chima enunciated, stressing each word with an accent resembling the British.

They all roared with laughter.

"And I am Lady Banke," Banke threw at them, imitating a curtsy, holding her skirt by the side, with her knees bent, and her head bowed.

The sound of their laughter rose, mixing with those close by. Just then, the peal of the bell rang out for the morning assembly to begin.

They made it to the new section, forming a line, while some of them stared at those who were now taking up where they stood last year. They lined up according to their heights, the shorter ones in front and the taller ones behind. The girls formed their lines, too.

Since it was a new session and no prefects had been selected yet, a teacher led the assembly. They sang praises and worship, recited the school anthem and pledge, and recited the national anthem and pledge, too. Then it was time for the principal, Mrs Ojo, to speak to them.

"Good morning, students. It is wonderful to see your faces again. Can we give a clap offering to God for bringing us together again without any incident?"

They gave it their all, as they clapped loudly. The principal had a hard time getting them to stop. They were excited.

She continued, "This is the beginning of a new session. Congratulations to those who got promoted. We have in our midst those who have just gotten into JSS1 after passing their promotion exams from primary school, and those who passed their Junior WAEC exams, and are now in SS1. Please clap for them."

Again, there was another round of applause.

"To those who are now in SS3, this is your last year here. You will have to study hard to prepare for your senior exams. You are aware that if you fail to prepare, you set yourself up for failure. I expect you to use your time wisely.

"To those who just got promoted to SS1, I have news for you. According to a new educational policy championed by the Education Board, students both in the sciences, commercial, and arts classes, will be made to take history classes."

A hum of conversation began immediately as the news produced stunned, wary looks.

Eze, who was standing behind Gregory, couldn't keep mum. "Haven't we done enough of social studies? We already know all we need to know," he complained, clearly not fancying the news.

Gregory didn't like it either, but preferred to stay quiet. He needed the principal to explain some more. There had to be a reason behind this.

"Quiet!" Mrs Ojo shouted.

The noise stopped abruptly.

"It is the board's decision owing to the fact that children in this time and age do not have an in-depth knowledge of the history of this country. We want an informed society, entrenched and imbued with the history and cultural values of this country. You will be taught with greater emphasis on these points. You would come to understand and appreciate your culture and what makes you who you are—a Nigerian.

"I expect you all to accept this as one of your core subjects. Also, I want to buttress that this is a subject that is on a par with other core subjects. Failure at it might cause a repeat for you. So take it seriously.

"Once more, you are all welcome. Strive to be obedient, responsible, and diligent students. Uphold the motto of this school: Aim high and work hard. Your teachers are available to see you through whatever mishaps. Also, my office is always open to everyone," she said.

The claps continued until she came down from the podium. The marching songs began and they took turns, line by line, making their way to their various classrooms.

CHAPTER THREE

By Wednesday, the students had settled in. The initial excitement had fizzled out. Both teachers and students had fallen into the rhythm and pattern of studies each day.

In SS1 commercial class, the students were rounding off their accounts class, which had involved two periods. Mrs Catherine Etomi had introduced the students to the world of accounting. Starting from the first period, the students were enraptured and drawn into the system of balancing numbers; a clear improvement from the world of business studies they had been immersed in during their junior secondary school days.

Gregory sat in the middle row, digesting every bit of information and taking down study notes in his new exercise book, while Mrs Catherine dictated from her study book right in front of her. Right from when Gregory had clocked ten, he knew he wanted to be an accountant. The few times he had stepped into a banking hall with either his father or mother had left an imprint in his mind. He loved to play with numbers. The cold, detached looks of the gentlemen and ladies—staff he observed in the banking halls—dressed in their neatly pressed suits and polished shoes, mesmerised him. He imitated the way the cashiers counted money at home. When he eventually got it right, counting just as fast as they could, he knew there was no turning back. He would become an accountant; and even take it up a notch to the level of a chartered accountant. He was ready to study hard to achieve it.

Thus, when the chime of the bell signified the end of the class and the beginning of the lunch break, Gregory wasn't ready for the class to end. As he watched Mrs Catherine depart, his face took on a countenance of unhappiness.

"Hey, cheer up, Greg!" Abiodun nudged Gregory's elbow from behind. "It's time for a well-deserved break. Phew! I'm so hungry."

"Me, too," Eze said.

Chima answered in the way of a yawn.

Eze laughed. "Abeg, close your mouth before you swallow us."

"Gregory, you know you can eat numbers for breakfast, lunch, and supper. If you aren't ready yet, keep imagining Mrs Catherine in front of the class. As for me, I am going to get fed." Chima got up sluggishly and walked out of the class, with Abiodun trailing behind him.

Eze drew Gregory up from his seat. "Come on, man, let's go get some doughnuts before they are all wolfed down by the hungry students of this school."

That elicited a loud chuckle from Gregory. He stood, breaking away from the spell of accountancy. Soon, they were all together in a queue, waiting to buy what they needed from the school canteen; the whole time eyeing the show glass which displayed pastries such as doughnuts, buns, puff puff, etcetera.

Some minutes later, they found a spot to relax, a bottle of coke in one hand, and a big piece of doughnut coated with sugar on the other.

"If nothing else gets to me to school every morning, this doughnut certainly will," Chima said playfully, sinking his teeth into the doughnut, the sugar forming an arc on his lips.

A round of laughter followed that.

"It's not just you, Chima. I totally agree," Banke added as she joined the fray, clutching her own doughnut with a bottle of Fanta.

The boys quickly created space for her on the large bench they sat on.

"No one makes them better than Mama Adaeze," she added.

"Even the doughnut at 'sit n relax' and 'crunchies' doesn't taste half this good," Abiodun joined in.

"You see why I say Adaeze is my wife. I will continue to woo her until she accepts me," Chima said.

The laughter now was rib-cracking.

"Oh boy! So you haven't gotten over her. She doesn't even see you at all. Musa has taken the spotlight," Gregory teased, clutching his sides as his stomach hurt.

"Who is Musa?" Chima asked, feigning anger, pulling the doughnut away from his mouth. "I just don't know what she sees in that tall, lean boy, eh." He got to his feet. "Look at me," he commanded, drawing attention to himself. "Am I not handsome enough?"

Other students were drawn into the conversation at this juncture, making fun of his statement.

"Maybe it's your bowlegs that's scaring her away. Can't you see Musa's slim legs?" Ope, a boy from SS1 science, jokingly asked.

Dismayed, Chima got up and walked to the centre of the canteen, staring at his legs. "I am Chima, the son of Chief Ogochukwu Onu. These bowlegs you see are no ordinary legs. They have been passed down from generation to generation. Announce a race between Musa and me and see what these legs can do. The winner shall have the heart of Adaeze," he pronounced, his eyes wide like saucers.

They all stared at him, laughing at the hilarity of the spectacle. Gregory stored the event in his memory to be used against Chima later in life.

The sound of the bell signified the end of the break. They all consumed their drinks fast and returned the bottles before heading back to class.

"What do we have for our next period?" Gregory asked.

"History is on," Banke said.

"Oh, no!" Gregory complained alongside Abiodun. "Just what do we need this for? I am not a historian."

"You can't possibly do accounts all day," Eze pointed out.

"Remember what the principal said. This subject is just as important as others. You have to take it seriously," Banke warned.

"Whatever!" Gregory huffed.

"Thank you, our school mother," Abiodun mocked.

Banke rolled her eyes as they strolled into their class.

CHAPTER FOUR

A tall, wide, and a heavy-set man with a tinge of mustache walked into the class a minute after they had settled in.

"Good afternoon, sir," they chorused, standing up to greet.

"Good afternoon, class. You may all sit down," he said, dropping his books on the table in front of the class. He grabbed a marker and wrote their subject on the blackboard in legible capital letters: HISTORY. Then, he swiveled to face the class. "This is our first class in our history lessons. I am Mr Julius. Can you all introduce yourselves so we can be better acquainted?"

They spent the next five minutes introducing themselves, one after the other.

"That's very good," Mr Julius said, clapping his hands. "Now we can move on. This class you are taking will be centred on the introduction of Nigeria and how it came to be. We shall give in-depth analysis; study personalities and characters; try to recapture the events in our minds; and immerse ourselves in the belief patterns, cultural diversifications, political structures, traditional systems, and the entire foundation that this country Nigeria is hinged upon.

"We will study and dissect it like we are foreigners; like the boys who love and talk about their football, like the girls who love and talk about their soap-operas!

"Also, I want to add that this would be an interactive and participatory class. It won't be one man calling the shots. Rather, you are all invited to take the shots," he said with a passionate grin.

Gregory turned to his right and caught Eze's eyes. They both wore the same looks.

Mr Julius was a man thoroughly wrapped in his world of Nigerian history. His passion oozed out of him in waves, enshrouding his students in its webs. He had them trapped in this. There was no going back.

To his left, Abiodun gave a sign with two fingers crossed together. Gregory groaned inwardly. It was a two period class. Escape had certainly flown out the door.

***

Hoofing back home later that day, Gregory found his mother sprawled on the couch, clutching her head. He dropped his bag and knelt down by her side. "Mum! Mum!" he said frantically. "What's wrong?"

The tears running down her cheeks struck him with dread. It was a silent cry, yet her face revealed the damage it had wrought. Her eyes were red and swollen, snot slipping out of her nose. Her lips trembled, and her face had bloated up. She had been crying for quite some time.

"What is it?" he tried again. "Is it Grandma?" A thought lashed into his mind, stifling and leaving him breathless. He couldn't bring himself to say the words. "Is she…?"

"No! No, my son!" his mother said, coming alive, clearly understanding what the question implied. "No, Gregory," she continued. "It just hurts to see her this way. It's like she is dead, you know. Dead to us! Dead to what's happening around her. She can't even recognise me—her daughter!"

"It's okay, Mum," Gregory said, wrapping his arms around her as she wailed. "Remember the doctor said it would be this way."

"It doesn't help! I'm torn apart. Go and look at her. She just sits there, not recognising or acknowledging anyone. Sometimes I wonder what runs through her mind the whole time. I can't bear to see her live like this. It hurts too much," she said, her voice breaking amidst hiccups.

No words could calm her. Gregory understood this. He held his mother for as long as she needed him while she sobbed and trembled in his arms.

After a while, the trembling ceased. His mother detached herself from his embrace and looked at him squarely in the face, clarity returning to her eyes. She sniffled. "You shouldn't see me like this."

"It's okay, Mum. Have you forgotten that I am your second husband?" he chided, handing his handkerchief over to her.

That drew a tiny smile on her lips. "Thank you, my husband," she said as she swung her legs to the floor to stand. "Let me get you your food."

"No, don't bother, Mum. Why don't you lie down and rest? I can take care of myself. I will even check on Grandma, too, okay."

"Thank you, my son. You are a good boy." She gave a tender pat to his head, then laid her full length on the couch, her emotions finally subsiding as she shut her eyes.

Gregory turned off the TV and ambled to his grandmother's room. She was fast asleep. He had a lot to do. He needed to wash his uniform and dig into his assignment from his history class on the civil war and how it came to an end.

CHAPTER FIVE

O n Friday, history class had taken over the two periods before lunch break.

"Why is it always two periods?" Gregory wondered aloud.

"Get used to it," Banke shouted from the front of the class.

"I hope you completed your assignment?" Abiodun asked.

"Of course, I did. My head is filled with coups and counter-coups, I could literally stage a coup against Mr Julius and his history class," Gregory said with a lop-sided grin.

"Oh, you must be Lieutenant Colonel Gregory Agwu of the Eastern region," Eze said drily.

Loud giggles rented the air. Gregory snorted loudly as their history teacher stepped into the class filled with laughing students. Mr Julius hovered at the doorway, observing them. The class fell silent at his stare. He walked in a couple of ticks later and dropped his books on the table, while the students got up to greet.

"Good day, class," he began. "I am glad to see you all in a jubilant mood today. It means your minds are relaxed and your mental state alert. We would definitely have an interesting conversation today. Please, sit down."

They all slid back to their seats at the gesture of his hand.

"Did you all complete your assignments?"

"Yes, sir!" they chorused.

"That's good! Please, submit them now."

They all got up to place their A4 papers filled with answers to the assignment on civil war on his table.

"Very good! Very good!" Mr Julius praised as they made their way back to their seats. "I'm glad you made the effort to work on your assignments.

"In our previous class, we talked about the colonisation of this country by the British and how Nigeria got its dependence in 1960. We learnt that a new constitution established a federal system with an elected prime minister in the person of Abubakar Tafawa Balewa, and a ceremonial head of state in the person of Nnamdi Azikiwe after a coalition was formed when neither of their parties—NCNC known as the National Council of Nigeria and the Cameroons which Azikiwe belonged to; and the NPC known as the Northern People's Congress which Balewa belonged to—failed to win a majority in the 1959 elections."

His voice thundered on.

"We established that in 1963, Nigeria became a republic, with Azikiwe president, and Balewa prime minister, which made him more powerful. As a country trying to capture its footing, Nigeria was plunged into a crisis owing to the major ethnic regions—the West controlled by the Yoruba, the East by the Igbo, and the North by the Hausa-Fulani—fighting over inequality, competitiveness, and economic balance.

"From your assignments, you would have discovered that it came to a head in January 1966, with the South complaining of northern domination and demanding secession, and the North fearing that the South were bent on capturing power because they were educationally advanced, after the collapse of order in the West following the fraudulent election of October 1965. Prime Minister Balewa and two regional premiers were murdered by a group of army officers in a bid to overthrow the federal government.

"A military administration was set up by Maj. Gen. Johnson Aguiyi Ironsi. But in July 1966, northern officers staged a counter-coup, and Aguiyi Ironsi was assassinated. Lieut. Col. Yakubu Gowon came to power. Who can tell me what happened afterwards?"

A couple of fingers shot up in the air. Mr Julius pointed at Banke.

She stood up. "Yakubu Gowon tried to hold a conference for pertinent issues to be discussed, but it was abandoned after a series of ethnic massacres in October."

"Very good," Mr Julius beamed. "Please, sit down. Who else can tell us what happened next?"

More fingers went up in the air. Gregory couldn't believe it. Apparently, they were all enjoying the class. Mr Julius had drawn them out. Excitement buzzed in the air.

This time, Abiodun was picked. "In 1967, the eastern delegation led by Lieut. Col. Odumegwu Ojukwu agreed to meet others at Aburi, Ghana. It failed to be a success due to differences over the interpretation of the accord."

"Good!" Mr Julius exclaimed; the passion in his eyes similar to a child waiting to unwrap his birthday present. The atmosphere was intense and turbo-charged. "Then what followed?"

Eze, who hardly uttered a word in class, raised his hand. "In May, the eastern region consultative assembly authorised Ojukwu to establish a sovereign republic, while the federal military government promulgated a decree, dividing the four regions which were now the: Eastern, Northern, Western, and Mid-western, into twelve states: six in the north, and three in the east, in order to stave the power of the regions."

Mr Julius marched down their line of seats, a whiff of excitement coming off of him.

Gregory could literally touch it. He had been drawn into the web. "The civil war had begun!" he cried dramatically with his right hand raised, his eyes fixed on a spot above the blackboard. Clearly, this was his stage; and they were his spectators.

"Who can briefly tell us how the civil war ran its course?"

Strangely, Gregory found himself doing something he didn't think would ever happen. *He was hypnotised, wasn't he?* Gregory lifted his hands.

Mr Julius gave him a nod of acknowledgement.

When Gregory stood up and opened his mouth, his voice came out in a squeaky tone. "Fighting broke out in early July," he began. "In August, the Biafran troops crossed the Niger, seized Benin City, and were on their way to Lagos before they were stopped at Ore. It didn't take a short while before the federal troops entered Enugu which was the provisional capital of Biafra. The next two years saw heavy fighting and an increasing number in the dead—both armies and civilians. The Organisation of African Unity tried to initiate peace talks, but they were unsuccessful."

"Clap for him," Mr Julius said.

They all clapped until it satisfied Mr Julius.

"The war lasted for two years, six months, one week, and two days; but left a lot of damage in its wake. The eastern region was brutalised, and left in charred ruins. Gowon, who was now a General, was able to bring the two sides together, integrating Biafra back into the country once again.

"In July 1975, Gowon fled to Great Britain, and the new head of state, Brig. Gen. Murtala Ramat Mohammed took over, initiating changes during his brief time in office such as starting off the process of moving the federal capital territory to Abuja. He was assassinated in February 1976 during an unsuccessful coup attempt. His top aide, Lieut. Gen. Olusegun Obasanjo became head of the government.

"Obasanjo did his best to return the country to civilian rule by promulgating a new constitution which invested a president to step into office only after winning one-fourth of the votes in two-thirds of the states in the federation.

"But do you know that a second civil war almost took place shortly after?" Mr Julius announced, his eyes growing wide, like he was about to reveal a deep secret.

A second world war! Gregory wondered. He had never heard of that.

Mr Julius continued. "Yes, a second civil war! It's not bandied about because the government refused to expose the fact that they couldn't keep a tight lid on the civilian rule, the oil boom, and the discovery of a new mineral resource in the North that almost disintegrated the country. They didn't want foreign nations thinking they couldn't handle their affairs. It was a hush-hush affair from 1979 to 1983. The country was in a great turmoil.

"But guess what? You get to know all about it in this class. Aren't you part of something special?" he disclosed.

"We are!" they agreed in a trance-like manner.

Clearly, his mouth dripped of honey.

"Class, say 'Jade,'" he commanded.

"Jade!" they chorused.

"In our next class, we will come to understand 'Jade'," Mr Julius said.

The bell tolled, and he rounded up his books, signifying the end of the class. As he strutted off, Gregory pictured him in a black flowing coat with a black hat sitting atop his forehead. What was missing was the beard. Mr Julius was a messenger from the late 1970s to the early 1980s, brought down to reveal secrets unbeknownst to them.

Gregory looked around him. They all wore the same hypnotic expressions. *What had just happened?*

CHAPTER SIX

The weekend flew by without any hitches. Gregory engaged in his share of duties at home. He did his laundry and even kept an eye on his grandmother when his mother went to the market. The highlight of the weekend was the football match played between Chelsea and Arsenal that ended in a draw. Abiodun came around to watch with him. They were both Arsenal fans. They ooh'd and aah'd for the entire ninety minutes plus extra time, and were disappointed at the outcome, eventually.

Monday morning had them arguing on their way to school over who was the better team with Chima and Eze—both Chelsea fans. They hadn't arrived at a truce before they arrived at school. Assignments were submitted and assessed, new topics in various subjects were introduced, and the students sunk their teeth into their books.

On Wednesday, at the appointed time, Mr Julius sauntered into the classroom.

"Good morning, sir."

"Good morning, class. You may take your seats."

They spent the first period taking a continuous assessment test. It was totally out of the blue. They had no option but to tackle it the best they could. At the end of the period, they submitted their papers; the unsure students murmuring under their breaths and wearing frowns, while the confident ones sported a cheery grin.

At the start of the second period, Mr Julius took his position at the front of the class. His voice boomed out.

"Today, we will begin our conversation concerning Jade, but first let's talk about the natural resource: oil. The first oil field in Oloibiri was created in 1958. Today, we have quite a number of oil fields. Operations began from 1963 to 1967. The early 1970s were referred to as the first oil boom. It dominated the economy, leading to a steady decline and eventual collapse in the agricultural sector and other sectors that held the Nigerian economy. In 1971, Nigeria became a member of the Organisation of Petroleum Exporting Countries (O.P.E.C). Commercial activities began between Nigeria and other foreign countries. Subsequently, revenue began flowing in.

"Also, in 1976, the number of states increased from twelve to nineteen. Out of the new states formed, the number of oil-producing states were: Rivers, Cross Rivers, and Ondo. The people of these states were not happy they didn't have a say in a mineral resource that was coming out of their land. The peace was fragile. A little rocking of the boat could tip it off. Also, they couldn't accept the domination by the northerners, who ruled them and their mineral resources. It was a very tense period. They wanted to have a say over what was theirs and not have the North enriched with what didn't belong to them."

Mr Julius paused, staring intensely at them. Then he continued, moving around the classroom as he spoke. "Several groups sprang up, challenging the arrangement and injustice of it all, however, they did it quietly. The oil was from their soil. It should equally enrich them, too. The fact that the northerners began owning oil wells, increased the level of injustice!"

They all sat in rapt attention as his voice resounded in the room, his Adam's apple bobbing in his throat.

"The party leaders used political power as an opportunity to gain access to public treasuries and distribute privileges to their followers. The groups formed, challenged the relevance of a democracy that could not produce leaders who would improve their lives and provide moral authority.

"The North tried to hold on to power. Call it a stroke of luck or whatever you might, but the North made a sterling discovery of a mineral resource known as 'Jade' in Kaduna. They tried to keep mum about it as they made plans to begin mining it. But soon, news of Jade reached the ears of others in various states. The fact that such knowledge had been placed on a tight lid was interpreted as a reckless, insensitive decision, leading to a strain between those in power, especially at the higher helm of affairs.

"The groups began requesting, again, for a separation of the regions which was what had led to the civil war in the first place. Those who had felt defeated over the loss of the war soon found their voices, clamouring for attention once again.

"At this point, the East felt they should be left with their oil, while the North were seeking also, to have sole access to their Jade, and wanted equally to go their separate way. The country could just as well be divided. It was a time of great distress, and pockets of fighting were reported all over the country, that almost led to a second civil war, but for the intervention of the traditional rulers, who helped navigate the murky waters, bringing its harried citizens back together."

The peal of the bell ringing led to the end of the class and the abrupt departure of Mr Julius.

Gregory remained seated, stunned. *Was that it? Was that all there was to the story? Could a situation this deep just have been swept under the carpet?* He vividly recalled the film: Black Diamond starring Leonardo DiCaprio and Djimon Hounsou. The horrors, bloodshed, violence, scheming, and desperation displayed in the movie over the mineral resource—diamond—had made it one of his favourites, and a best-selling movie all over the world.

There had to be more to this. Gregory felt empty. A great discontent and dissatisfaction assailed him. There had to be answers somewhere. *But where would he find it?* For the very first time, he wasn't looking forward to a bottle of coke and doughnut. History had taken root underneath his skin.

CHAPTER SEVEN

From that moment, Gregory felt a deep restlessness. He became a self-appointed researcher. During lunch breaks, he settled in front of one of the computers in the library, googling results for Jade in reference to the almost second civil war, but found no concrete information. He scoured the history books too, but also came up blind.

During Friday's lessons, he couldn't help but lift up a finger during class, to ask Mr Julius if that was all there was to the story.

There had to be more!

The first civil war was widely known and was still talked about up till date. Writers wrote stories using the background of the civil war. Films were produced in the same way. Ojukwu was still celebrated and honoured as a national hero. Who were the heroes of this almost second civil war? There had to be answers somewhere.

The lack of enough information exasperated him.

Mr Julius wore a troubled expression for a few minutes while he pondered what to say. "I understand your feelings, Gregory. I was once where you are now. As a passionate historian who knows this country like the back of my hand, I endured sleepless nights wondering what had happened. Because of the many blank spaces in the story, this event is not taught in history classes because it will produce the frustrations that you are now experiencing.

"I only want to believe that those in power from 1979 to 1983 felt it very expedient to put this information under wraps; probably as a matter of national security. In fact, we may never know what truly happened, unless a new source of revelation resurfaced. Who knows, a group of archaeologists may uncover some ancient scrolls or journals that may shed more light," he joked, producing short outbursts of laughter from all of them.

"The populace at that time, which includes your parents and your grandparents, if they are still alive, do not even have the specifics. No one knows the nitty-gritty. All I can say is that we are all being protected from things that are surely above us. Accept things as they are and come to a place of rest with it like I did," he added.

The last statement chugged Gregory's memory. His mother had been born in Kaduna before her parents relocated to the east. She was born in 1977! This was 2015. He quickly did the math. She was thirty-eight now, which meant she was two-years old in 1979. Would she have the answers? Or probably grandmother?

But Grandmother had Alzheimer's!

Even if she knew anything, would she be able to recall any of it? Grandma's Alzheimer's was at stage four. It was described as being at a mild or early stage. It wasn't so far gone yet, although there had been the occasional withdrawal from conversations and an increase in the clear signs of dementia. The picture looked bleak.

**

During the weekend, Gregory kept at his research at home, online. As nothing still turned up, his frustrations mounted. He rose from his chair, pensive. He picked his way to the kitchen, where his mother was preparing Onugbu soup for lunch. The aroma hit him even before he made his entrance.

"Mmm…this smells nice! My stomach is rumbling already," he said.

His mother turned around from the cooker. "Thanks, my son." Rivulets of sweat were dripping down her face. "It's almost ready."

"I can't wait, Mum," Gregory said, hovering at the doorway.

"Just a few more minutes, okay," she said, as she checked the pot of water which she intended using to prepare the semovita.

"Mum," he began. "Can I ask you a question?"

"Go on," she urged as she returned to stirring the pot of soup.

"Do you know about what took place from 1979 to 1983?"

"What do you mean?" she asked, her brows furrowed.

"I mean concerning the war that almost broke out after the civil war."

She whipped around. "How do you know that?"

Gregory walked into the kitchen and placed his hands on the counter, his gaze intense. "We were taught in our history class."

"Really? I wasn't taught. The little I know I gleaned from snatches of conversations between your grandma and my late father."

What! Gregory's hopes developed wings. "So what did you hear?" he asked excitedly, his curiosity apparent.

"Whoa! Cool down, son! Not much, I must say. It wasn't anything new. The country was thrown into chaos due to the discovery of Jade. Upon closer examination, it was found to be Jadeite. Greed almost took over, but the traditional rulers stepped in and normalcy returned."

"Is that all?"

"Yes! That's all. What else were you expecting?"

"There has to be more, na!" he complained. "It couldn't just have ended that way!"

His mother laughed aloud at how he sounded like a child throwing a tantrum. "That is all we know. Ask your father and he will tell you the same, too."

"What of Grandma? Wouldn't she know something?"

"No!" she said, dropping the spoon. "Do not disturb her. I know you when you make up your mind about something. Let this drop."

"But, Mum, what if she knows? The doctor said it's just at its early stage. She may still remember."

"If she knew anything, wouldn't she have mentioned it all these years? Don't you think so? Now, don't disobey me," his mother threatened, pointing her finger at him.

The sound of the water boiling for the semovita drew her attention away. Gregory walked out, disappointed. He had to find a way to move on from this.

CHAPTER EIGHT

I n class the following week, Gregory couldn't concentrate. His mother knew him too well. When he made up his mind concerning anything, he stuck to it, committing himself wholeheartedly. This was what he felt about accounting. And now, he felt the same about Jade.

He was a man on a mission. He needed to find closure or he wouldn't be himself. Gregory sat lost in thought, thinking of a way forward, when a word spoken by his mother whipped through his head.

She had mentioned Jadeite.

Was it the same as Jade, or were they two different things? He had to find out. He was out of the class the second the bell rang for lunch break, lunch being at the back of his mind again.

"Hey! Where are you off to?" Abiodun called out.

Gregory had no time to spare. He rushed to the library, relieved to find an empty spot in front of a computer. He pulled up the internet browser and typed: *JADE*. When the results popped out and his understanding grew as he perused it, he struggled to stay calm. One of the results read thus:

Jade is a rough, compact, typically green gemstone found in the earth's crust, present in metamorphic terrains. It can be described as an ornamental mineral mostly known for its green varieties. It can be referred to as either of two different minerals: Nephrite—a silicate of calcium and magnesium, or Jadeite—a silicate of sodium and aluminum. It is found in rocks that have been subjected to high pressure below the earth's surface.

Did it mean that the mineral in the Jade discovered in Kaduna was Jadeite which is the rarer of the two minerals? He read on:

Jadeite has a vitreous lustre, is transparent-opaque, with a variety of colours such as white, emerald green, apple green, red, brown, blue, deep green, and black varieties coloured by iron known as 'Chloromelanite'. It is used in making jewelry, decorative objects, and even weapons and sculptures.

It is equally the most expensive mineral in the world! Gregory's eyes bulged. It could generate more income than oil. Gregory felt more determined now. He had to find the truth. Grandma was his last hope. If nothing came out of it, he would have to go the way of Mr Julius and the others.

But just how would he go about it?

The answer came to him almost immediately. It was right in front of him. A feral grin stretched his lips as he rubbed his hands together in excitement. He would eventually get what he needed.

On the way home from school, Gregory opened up to his friends and enlisted their help with his plan.

"Oh, boy o! When did you become this interested in history?" Eze asked.

"Are you bored with numbers already?" Abiodun added.

"No! No!" Gregory lifted his hands. "I just feel the need to get to the bottom of this."

"Gregory Agwu, is it our new status of senior boys that's getting to your head? What makes you think you can unravel what Almighty Mr Julius couldn't? What if it yields nothing?" Chima stressed.

"Then I would lick my wounds. Come on, guys! Help me out," he pleaded. "Take it as an adventure."

"Okay," they all agreed. "We can search for it tomorrow."

***

The next day after school, they began wandering the streets, looking for what they needed. They searched every nook and cranny. They even checked various jewelry stores the following day and the day after, hoping they would be lucky enough to find it at an affordable price, but it yielded nothing.

At the last stop, they found something very close to what they needed, but the price tag was ridiculous. It was going at a price of 150,000 naira. What they had come up with was 2,500 naira. Gregory found it difficult to let go of the piece. He could see the answer before his very eyes.

He fell to his knees, pleading with the manager of the store, while his friends tried to pull him up. Only a threat from the manager to visit their school the next day and report them—in order to find out what four senior secondary school students wanted to do with such an expensive piece of jewelry—forced Gregory to leave. Outside, the boys turned on him.

"What is wrong with you, eh?" Abiodun asked in a huff.

"Do you want to get us in trouble?" Eze chipped in.

Only Chima kept quiet, deep in thought.

"Guys, I am sorry, okay. That's the closest we have come to finding it."

"At 150k! Something is wrong with you," Abiodun said. "In fact, just don't say another word and pray hard that the manager doesn't make good his threat."

"I think we need to involve Banke. This is a woman's thing," Chima spoke up, coming out of his thoughts.

Gregory's face brightened. "Why didn't I think of that? It would have saved us a lot of time."

When they informed Banke during lunch break the next day, she sent them a strange look. "Are you sure of this?"

A nod from them was all the answer she needed.

Banke led them all the way from G.R.A to Ikeja Underbridge after school. They crisscrossed streets, sweating under the hot tropical heat as they struggled for space. With the throng of pedestrians pressing in from all sides, walking with hurried steps, their gaze focused on something ahead, as if what they needed was right in front of them. They finally came to a Mallam standing by a corner.

"Are you sure? Is it safe?" Gregory asked.

Banke snorted in derision. "Isn't it too late for this question, Mr Cautious? My elder sisters buy from him so I know him well."

She trudged ahead while they followed behind.

"*As-salaam-alaikum*," she greeted.

The Mallam turned to her. "*Wa-alaikum-salaam.*"

Banke pressed closer to him, whispering while he zeroed his full attention to their conversation.

"Did you say green?" he asked, re-confirming.

"Yes," she said.

The Mallam walked into his house, which was a ramshackle made up of logs of wood, and piles of zinc, which served as the roof. The structure was slightly tilted to one side. Two minutes later, the Mallam came out bearing a tray.

They all peered closer, staring at the contents littered all over. The display of greenish ornaments enraptured Gregory.

"Pick one fast," Banke said in a haste. "We need to get home as soon as possible."

Gregory pointed to a silver bracelet with a green stone at the centre. The idea had come to him during the search for Jade online. He had stumbled upon an article that highlighted the level of fraud associated with Jade. Some dubious jewelry merchants sold green gemstones which weren't Jade to unsuspecting buyers, raising concerns about how to identify a true Jade gemstone. This piece of information had played right into his hands, providing an avenue for him. They completed the transaction and hurried away; the others, glad to be done with it.

"Thank you, guys. You are clearly the best friends anyone could hope for," Gregory said.

"Let's just hope it produces the desired effect," Abiodun replied.

"Step one is over. On to step two," Gregory spoke out loud, his shoulders squared up in confidence.

CHAPTER NINE

Gregory stepped into his house, a strategy already in place in his mind.

"Gregory," his mother called as she rushed to the living room from the kitchen, having heard the door opening. "What happened? Why are you late?"

"Mum…"

"Are you all right?" she continued, scanning him from his head to his toes.

"Mum, I am fine. We were given a tough math assignment, so my friends and I stayed back in school to figure it out," he lied, although not pleased with himself for doing so.

"Oh!" his mother said, her hands to her chest. "I was so worried. I wish your school would change their no phone policy. It would have saved me this headache."

"It's okay, Mum. I am here now," Gregory said, hugging her. "How is Grandma today?"

"Oh, your Grandma is better today," she said, the edges of her mouth showing the beginnings of a smile. "I will have her come sit with us for dinner instead of eating alone in the room. Now, go take a shower."

Gregory couldn't help smiling as he turned to his room. All was going well so far. Grandma had returned to herself. The time was apt.

He had a quick shower and was seated at the dining table a few minutes before 6:00 p.m. His mother was holding on to Grandma as she took steps towards the dining table.

"Good evening, Grandma," Gregory greeted, standing up to hug her.

"How are you, Greg?" Grandma asked, a light of recognition in her eyes.

Gregory couldn't help it. He held her tight. Grandma always called him Greg, never using Gregory. He had never been happier hearing her call him that now. "I'm fine, Grandma. Please take your seat," he urged, guiding her to a chair, while his mother went back to the kitchen, returning with their plates of food.

Dinner was yam pepper soup with goat meat. It was a rule to keep quiet during meals, but the rule was discarded tonight, especially since Gregory's father was out of town on a business trip. They chatted on, filling Grandma in on all that had taken place. They talked through the washing of the dishes, to when they settled down in the living room to watch a family sitcom on TV.

Gregory observed the atmosphere until he was pretty sure the mood was relaxed, and Grandma was very comfortable. "I will be right back," he announced, getting up to go to his room. He took out the gift, wrapped in a wrapping sheet from his school bag, and drew a quick breath.

It was time!

With his heart hammering against his ribcage, he walked back to the living room and sat beside her.

"Grandma, I have something special for you. A gift," he said, showing her what was in his right palm.

"What?" his mother and grandmother said aloud.

"*Chim o!*" his grandmother choked out, her eyes watering. "You got a gift for me."

"Yes, Grandma. Something to make you smile and forget all that has happened."

"*Ewo!*" she said. "God bless you, my grandson," she said, the tears threatening to spill down her cheeks.

"Grandma, open it first and see, na," Gregory said with a light chuckle.

"*Ngwanu, Nne! Mepeya,*" Gregory's mother encouraged her.

With shaky hands, Grandma began unwrapping the gift. Gregory couldn't sit still. He stood up, panicking inside. If this didn't get her to speak, if at all she knew something, it would mean the end of his search. He hoped his mother would forgive him for his mischief.

When the gift was revealed, both his mother and grandmother gasped aloud. It was a beautiful bracelet. Gregory hadn't even noticed its beauty until tonight. It was the verdant stone at the centre that had held him captive. If this failed, he could find happiness in the fact that he had gotten something beautiful for his grandmother.

"Where did you get the money to buy this?" his mother asked curiously.

"I have been saving my pocket money."

"Oh *nwam*," his mother said, walking up to him. "You have done well."

Grandma lifted it up from the sheet, turning it over. Her eyes caught the sight of the green stone, the light from the chandelier reflecting on it, making it glow. Her reaction was instantaneous. She drew back, her eyes expanding in their sockets and her pupils pin-pointed with dark concentration, her mouth agape.

"*Nne*, what is it?" his mother asked, alarmed.

Grandma remained in that posture, her head bent low.

His mother pointed an accusatory finger at him. "What is happening here?" she barked.

"I don't know, Mum," he replied, still trying to play out his part. He had initiated this, but Grandma's reaction was scaring him. He just wasn't showing his fear yet.

Suddenly, Grandma's head shot up. She fixed her gaze on Gregory for so long he couldn't bear to look at her. In a shaky voice, she asked, "Where did you get this?"

"I bought it for you, Grandma... from a Mallam."

"Mallam!" his mother's shocked voice rose an octave.

"This is Jade," Grandma announced. "This is a Jade stone."

Gregory looked at her, dazed as he tried to avoid his mother's accusing stare. No, she didn't. She couldn't... Did she just say 'Jade'?

CHAPTER TEN

Gregory's mind was absent during class. Even when Mrs Catherine walked in for the accounts class, he paid no attention. How could he? When his mind kept returning to the events of last night.

After Grandma's announcement that the stone was Jade, she had broken into quiet sobs. They couldn't get her to stop. Eventually, his mother took Grandma into her room and gave her a sedative to help her sleep.

When his mother returned to the living room, she was livid. She called him irresponsible. She had seen through his gimmick, and his disobedience infuriated her.

Gregory could barely catch a wink of sleep that night. Now that he learned Grandma held knowledge of a hidden history—she wouldn't react that way if she knew nothing—he wished he hadn't taken his probing that far. He started a puzzle he couldn't finish, leaving him deeply involved, frustrated, and at a loss as to what his next step would be.

His friends tried to cheer him up, but their efforts were futile. Gregory carried his despair and frustrations home. It was a great effort to open the door and step into his house.

Gregory's mother was on the couch, facing the door. She observed his entrance as their eyes locked.

"Good afternoon, Mum."

"Welcome, my son."

The mention of 'my son' filled Gregory with relief. Did it mean she already forgave him?

"I'm sorry about what happened yesterday, Mum."

"It's okay. You are forgiven, but don't do that again. It's wrong. When you are through with your food, your grandma wants to see you."

See him! Was there still hope?

Gregory exited his stunned state, hurried to his room to take a shower, and went back to their kitchen to eat his meal. Shortly after, he knocked on his grandmother's door.

"Come in," came her faint answer.

Upon opening the door, he found Grandma seated in the armchair beside her bed. Gregory sat down on the bed, facing her. "Grandma, please, I am sorry if I caused you any hurt last night. It wasn't my intention."

Her stare carried an intense heat that bore a hole in his chest. "It is okay, my grandson. Thank you for the gift. I appreciate it."

Gregory let out a sigh of relief. "Do you like it?"

"Of course," she said passionately. "It brought back memories long hidden. I absolutely love it."

"Memories?   Really,   Grandma!   What memories?" Gregory asked.

Grandma fixed him again with yet another intense look. "Your mother informed me about some events taking place at school. Do you care to share with me?"

Gregory understood that this was a test he had to pass. If Grandma had kept whatever knowledge she had hidden for years without divulging it to anyone, she needed a good enough reason to open up now. It was apparent she was privy to some knowledge.

So, Gregory opened his mouth to speak. He began with his aloofness towards the history class, how Mr Julius drew them all in, and how he started taking part in the teachings concerning the civil war and the second war that almost broke out after it.

"Grandma, I have surprised myself by being this involved. But if there is a story here, and I believe there is, it must be told. It is a part of the Nigerian history. We can't just let it fizzle away. It should be passed from generation to generation; and if possibly, celebrated," he said.

Gregory wasn't good at speeches, but he believed he had outdone himself here. Grandma turned her face to the ceiling, deep in thought. His mother knocked before entering the room and sat down beside him, her hands over his. Gregory appreciated the touch.

"Ngozi, can you pull up my old trunk from underneath the bed?" Grandma said to his mother.

Gregory and his mum both got down on their knees. They raised the flaps of the duvet so they could see the trunk and heaved it from underneath the bed. A cloud of dust hovered in the air. Gregory had a little coughing fit to clear his throat.

Grandma pointed at the trunk. "Please, open it."

His mother removed the unlocked padlock that had rusted away, and pulled up the metal latch. Gregory stared, amazed at its contents. It was filled with old paraphernalia. He sighted old newspaper clippings, their edges gray with age; a handful of hand woven thread for knitting and tatting, and long needles for sewing; a handful of cookery books, an old bible commentary, and even an old pair of scissors.

They pushed the trunk closer to Grandma. She bent low, her gaze fixed on the right side of the trunk as if she knew exactly what she was doing. She pushed things aside and dug her hand to the bottom of the trunk, fingers closing around something.

Gregory held his breath as she drew her hand out of the trunk, clasped around a piece of cloth wrapped to an unidentified object. His heartbeat quickened, gaze centred to the movement of her fingers while she untied it. Anticipation prickled his nape, along with the sharp intake of breath from his mother. In these few agonizing seconds, they had forgotten how to breathe.

When Grandma pulled back the last piece of fabric, a stone stared at them.

Was it a stone?

Gregory had visited the Olumo rock in Abeokuta with his classmates on an excursion. He suddenly remembered the look of it.

Could it…Could it be what he was thinking?

Gregory sprang up from the bed to give it a closer look. He stared at his grandmother, his eyes asking the silent question: *can I touch it?*

At Grandma's nod of affirmation, Gregory ran his hands over it. A ripple of shock went through him. It felt like a rock! Grandma turned it around, and a green gemstone embedded in the rock stared at him. He touched it. It was cold, smooth, and soap-like.

Gregory looked stunned. Amazed. Confused. Perplexed. Overwhelmed. His mother shouted. Grandma had Jade in its raw form.

For it to have come out of this old trunk, there must be a history behind it. He looked at Grandma and caught her mischievous wink. He couldn't help but think that Grandma looked like an old witch from a cartoon who had just opened her chest of hidden secrets.

"Grandma..."

CHAPTER ELEVEN

Grandma's revelation of the Jade rocked them to the very core. Gregory wanted her to get right to the nitty-gritty of the story.

But there was a catch.

Grandma had fallen in love with Mr Julius' personality and his desire to know the truth. She wanted him present when she unraveled the mystery.

It was a Wednesday, so Gregory waited till the end of the history class before he approached Mr Julius in the staff room.

"What?" Mr Julius cried out in disbelief. "She is privy to what happened?"

"Yes," Gregory replied. He revealed everything except his grandmother's possession of the Jade. He also explained her health condition.

It put a damper on Mr Julius' spirit. He looked concerned. "Are you sure she would be able to cope? Wouldn't it be too stressful for her to relive all that happened?"

"It worries us, too. I am only telling you so we can take it easy with her and not rush her. Let her take it at her own pace."

Mr Julius retreated into silence before he spoke again. "Do you know the implication of this, Gregory? This would be a first-hand story of what transpired years ago. It may open doors we never truly expected."

The optimism and candor of Mr Julius swept him away. They agreed to meet up when school closed for the day.

***

Gregory got home as soon as he could. He managed to explain what had happened to his friends before getting home.

"Yay!" they exclaimed happily. "The plan worked."

"We owe this to Banke," Chima pointed out. "We must celebrate her tomorrow with extra doughnuts."

They all laughed hard.

Gregory rushed through his shower and meal like a cyclone.

"Calm down," his mother said. "Your grandma isn't running away."

Gregory crept up to his mother, a fixated look on his face. "Is she ready?"

A look of worry swept across his mother's features. "She is ready; but I am still concerned. I hope the excitement won't be too much for her."

"Don't worry, Mum," he reassured. "We wouldn't push her. We are all here for her, okay."

Just then, a knock sounded at the door. It was Mr Julius.

"Hello Ma'am. I am Mr Julius, Gregory's history teacher," he said after stepping into the living room. "Thanks so much for having me."

Gregory's mother let out a soft laughter. "You are welcome, but the thanks should go to my mother and not to me. I am not the one in the spotlight. She is the one pulling the strings here. Please, sit down, and let me inform her of your presence."

A few minutes later, they were all in Grandma's bedroom. She felt more comfortable there. She sat on her armchair while Gregory brought in chairs from the dining room.

"I never knew one day I would have to tell this story," she began. "But I see the yearning for the truth in my grandson's eyes. It is what compelled me to speak before I lose all my memories to Alzheimer's."

Grandma's hands trembled at this point—a giveaway to her apprehension about her sickness.

They all saw it.

Gregory's mother tried to speak, but Grandma quickly waved her off and continued. "Some parts will elicit joy. Others will elicit pain and hurt. But no matter the emotion involved, I will tell it all. This is how it began:

"When my husband came for my hand in marriage in 1975, I was ready to leave my parents and start a family of my own. The only issue was that my husband, Mr Chijioke Nwankpa, lived in Kaduna state. His parents had relocated to Kaduna when he was ten-years old, but they had decided to have their son return to his homeland to get a wife, instead of marrying a northerner. Chijioke was obedient to them and made the journey across the River Niger to find a wife. This was how I met my husband when I was twenty-five..."

***

The end of the civil war in 1970 left everyone in a state of shock. The tragic loss of lives and the wanton destruction left in its wake, left a sour taste in the mouth, even after five years had gone past. It brought to the fore the realisation that time was precious, and whatever time that was left, needed to be spent making the most of it, and being surrounded by loved ones.

Chinenye was in this place of self-awareness. She needed to feel whole; a fresh start. She didn't want to live in fear anymore. The fighter jets no longer flew in the air, their wings hovering like a shadow of death. So why allow her mind to be wrapped in fear? They called it the perils of war; games of the mind. But she wouldn't have it anymore.

Yes, they had been greatly affected. Sadly, her brother, Obiora, the first son of the family, had passed away. She could recall very vividly the day

Obiora walked out of the house, determination and a sense of purpose evident on his face. He was going to join the Biafran Army. Her parents were filled with pride, and her father never failed to mention it to anyone who cared to listen about the family's effort in fighting the war. When they received the news of Obiora's death—he had been killed in a bomb explosion—it was like life had been sucked out of them. The fact that they wouldn't receive his body for proper burial left them heart-broken.

But surely, five years was enough time to grieve. Obiora was gone. It was time to move forward. No more will the curtains be drawn, enveloping the house in semi-darkness. No more will they talk in whispers, or walk tiptoeing for fear their footsteps will be heard.

Her mother stared at her strangely, her father shook his head whenever she admonished her siblings and encouraged them to play and lose their self-restraint. Gradually a chuckle morphed into a quiet laugh, and Chinenye realised they were making progress. Yes, they will overcome this.

One beautiful Saturday morning, her father was sitting at the verandah, enjoying the cool morning breeze. His transistor radio was tuned to Radio Nigeria, as he listened in rapt attention to the early morning news. When a sudden noise broke his reverie, Pa Chinenye turned in annoyance, and realised it was his friend, Pa Okorie, calling out to him. He had failed to hear his approaching footsteps.

"Ah, Pa Okorie, *I ḅọla chi?*"

Pa Okorie had joined him on the long bench. "Yes, my friend, I woke up well. I can see your day is going well," he said, as they shook hands.

Pa Chinenye chuckled. "It will definitely get better with you here. Who is there?" he called out.

Chinenye rushed out to answer her father's call. At the sight of Pa Okorie, her face brightened. "Pa, good morning," she greeted.

"Good morning, my daughter."

"*Bia*, bring that keg of palm wine that Uche dropped off this morning, and some kolanut," Pa Chinenye said.

"Okay, Papa."

Chinenye soon returned with the items which she placed on a table in front of them. The friends toasted with the palm wine.

"May we live long! May we see our grandchildren! May our country, Nigeria, never see another war! May peace reign!" Pa Chinenye prayed.

"Amen!" Pa Okorie said.

They both drank from their cups, enjoying the taste of the palm wine.

Pa Chinenye cleared his throat. Uhm…Uche is best supplier of palm wine."

"Oh yes! And it has wet my throat enough to be able to relay the good news I have for you."

Surprised, Pa Chinenye asked, "What good news?"

"A responsible, young man wants to ask for your daughter's hand in marriage."

There was a short silence, before Pa Chinenye spoke in a voice that was thick with emotions. "It's been really difficult trying to be normal again. When I remember all those we have lost, especially my son Obiora, I am filled with so much pain. However, life goes on. My daughter is twenty-five, and ripe for marriage. Let that young man and his family come to knock on my door."

The traditional marriage was a quiet affair. Chijioke's parents were in Kaduna. Only his father's kinsmen accompanied him. However, Chinenye was a happy bride. She had morphed into being a wife, and was anxious to begin her new life. When Chijioke informed her a week later that it was time to leave, she said her final good-bye to her family.

They made their journey to Kaduna with a mammy wagon. It was pretty tedious. They were cramped together with people of different tribes. Tensions were still high and the atmosphere was wrought with bitterness. They were all wary of each other. Some still looked clothed in a garment of violence, their bodies held stiff in a state of alertness, eyes darting back and forth, clouded in unhinged madness, which gave them away. The oil of violence had not completely been washed away. Chinenye stayed close to Chijioke; never leaving his side.

When they arrived in Kaduna, they still underwent another trip to Kaduna North; a local government area. They were headed to the town of Doka—the headquarters of Kaduna North Local Government.

Doka was a cosmopolitan city with ninety per cent Hausa Fulani and a Christian minority. The people lived in compact villages in hills or dense forests. Houses were made of mud with grass roots that cover the outer porch, and the granary which held the season's harvest. Each village was a clan community separated into extended family compounds. The village headman handled village affairs with the help of the council of elders.

The people were subsistence farmers. They grew millet, maize, guinea corn, and beans. They also reared goats, sheep, chickens, dogs, and even horses. Agriculture was the mainstay, but they did a bit of hunting and trading.

It was in one of these family compounds that they made their home, alongside Chijioke's parents. Chijioke's father had relocated to Kaduna to serve a trader, Alhaji Danladi, who taught him the tricks of the trade and gave him a house in his compound.

Chijioke had learned the trade from his father and now, traded in leather goods, plastics, and ceramics. Chinenye sometimes helped out in his shop. After her arrival, he took up a bit of farming. He had purchased a plot of land before getting married, but hadn't the time to till the soil.

As a young couple, they looked forward to having a child as soon as possible. But when six months had gone by and there was no sign of a baby forthcoming, Chinenye became restless. Chijioke decided to expand his business in order to accommodate her. He gave her money to buy some fabrics and start a business of her own in his shop, which would keep her busy. She went along with the idea.

She soon began selling knit fabrics and some Igbo George wrappers, which she had purchased from a well-known Igbo trade in Kaduna. Soon, she had an array of beautiful fabrics, resplendent in shiny colours on display. She began making sales and her friendships grew. She also started learning the language of the people so she could communicate better.

Chinenye's customers were mainly Igbo women who lived in the area. So you could imagine her surprise when a woman walked into her shop, dressed in a Jilbab—a long and loose fit coat covering the entire body that is characteristic of a Hausa woman.

"*Sannu*," she greeted.

"*Sannu kadai*," Chinenye responded, wondering what she was doing here.

She began sifting through the fabrics while Chinenye looked on in shock. *Was she really going to buy it, sew it, and wear it?* She hadn't seen a Hausa woman dressed in the tradition of another culture. She must have worn my emotions on her sleeve because when she looked at her to comment on one of the fabrics, she stared for a few seconds before bursting out in a loud laugh.

"Oh… I wish I could buy it, but I can't. I am only admiring them. If it offends you, I will leave," she said, good-naturedly.

Chinenye grinned. "It's okay. You can admire them." She felt drawn to the woman's openness. "My name is Chinenye Nwankpa."

"I am Alhaja Amina Muhammed."

Chinenye and Amina started off a friendship which made them feel more like sisters and Amina made being in a foreign land fun for Chinenye. She was the wife of a very rich man in the community and was forbidden to work. So every day, she would spend a few hours with her. They were never tired of each other's company. Conversation flowed freely between them. She educated Chinenye more about Hausa culture, and Chinenye did the same with the Igbo culture. Although Alhaja Amina was far older than her and had her only child—an eighteen-year-old daughter—schooling abroad, she took her under her wings and made her feel loved.

Chinenye's dream finally became a reality in 1977. She fell pregnant, and gave birth to her daughter, Ngozi. Alhaja Amina was there for her because her mother-in-law was bedridden with a sickness that had defied all kinds of treatment. Sadly, she passed away in 1978. Their friendship grew through the stormy tumults of the political atmosphere. And in 1979 when Shehu Shagari was elected into office, her husband was elected as the local government chairman of Kaduna North.

They danced and celebrated his victory. Chinenye was happy for her friend. Her husband, Alhaji Ali, was very excited at his appointment. He bragged about the things he would do and the developmental change that would take place across the region. She believed in him because of his wife, her friend. She had a good heart and would steer her husband on the right course. The future looked bright.

***

In Grandma's room, they were all enraptured by the story. When Grandma stopped abruptly, Gregory's mother rushed to her side.

"*Nne*, are you okay?"

"Yes," she replied tiredly. "Let's continue tomorrow."

His mother shooed them out of the room to give his grandmother a space to breathe.

In the living room, Mr Julius turned to Gregory with a mystified expression. "Is this real? If not, pinch me so I can wake up from this dream."

"It is very real, Mr Julius. I can't wait to learn what happened next."

"Me, too!" Mr Julius added with a feeling of nostalgia. "Me, too."

CHAPTER TWELVE

The next day, after school had closed for the day, Grandma was ready to pick up from where she stopped. They all gathered once more in her room. She began with a twinkle in her eyes.

✳✳✳

The town of Doka took on a new atmosphere with the appointment of Alhaji Ali. Being the headquarters of Kaduna local government, it was a very busy town in 1980.

Alhaja Amina, got immersed in the activities set out for the chairman's wife; mostly hosting. With the influx of people wanting to ingratiate themselves to the new chairman, or seek favours, her daily visits were no longer feasible, as her house became a beehive of activities. Yet, she managed to see Chinenye at least once every week. Chinenye felt touched that she valued their friendship that much; and made sure to always be there for her whenever she needed her.

Chinenye's duties as a wife, mother, and caregiver to her father-in-law who had aged overnight after the death of his wife, had her wrapped up in her world. Her husband, Chijioke, had begun taking business trips outside Doka in a bid to expand his business and make more money. Thus, she had no idea when 'it' started; the events that would put Doka on the sands of time.

Alhaji Suleiman, the wealthiest man in Doka, was a farmer who exported produce such as millet, maize, and guinea corn to other states. He owned hectares of land; such that a huge chunk of it had not been cultivated. It was filled with gigantic trees and dense vegetation. Alhaji Suleiman was eighty-six-years old, and was well known for his wisdom, generosity, and quest for peace. He had a very large household, his extended compound being one of the largest in the town. His pride was in his twenty-five sons.

Alhaji Suleiman loved to lie down in front of his mud house, late every evening, to watch the happenings in his compound. He enjoyed watching the little ones run around as they played and laughed with child-like abandon. When they tried to get close to him, and either one of his ten wives tried to chase them away for fear of disturbing him, he always reproached them gently. He enjoyed the company of the little ones. Their quick chatter and innocent laughter filled him with warmth. He had a strong feeling that the times he spent with them, even though he didn't get to talk much, helped to elongate his life span.

Another scene Alhaji Suleiman loved to gaze upon was the young men in his compound. The strength of their youth—virility and agility, reminded him of his early days. At the end of the day's work, when they returned from the farm in groups, laughing and talking loudly, he always had a smile for them as they came to him to pay their respects. They were all both his offspring and products of his offspring; a continuation of his bloodline.

One day, an idea struck him. He wondered why he hadn't thought of it earlier. He had been content with what he had, but with the increase in his household, there was a need to expand. In fact, he needed to do so before he breathed his last, so he could give his final words to avoid future family squabbles. *A wise man knew to set his affairs in order.* Thus, he requested to see his eldest son, Mustapha.

Mustapha rushed to his father's hut. He knew that death was fast approaching for his father. He hoped it wasn't today, for he wasn't prepared to let his father go yet.

Alhaji Suleiman wasted no time stating his intentions, his words coming out in muffled tones. "It is time for me to share my lands amongst my sons."

Mustapha was taken aback. "But father, you have already done so!"

"No! I mean the lands that haven't been cultivated. Bring me the deeds so I can share them immediately."

It should have been a propitious time for Mustapha, but his heart was heavy and filled with sorrow. His father had just spoken like someone who was carrying out his last wish.

Mustapha gathered the documents together and took it to his father. For the next two weeks, his father, with his help, shared the lands amongst his sons and grandsons. None was left out; except those who hadn't been born yet. The twenty-five sons thanked their father; grateful for his kindness. Alhaji Suleiman felt peace in his heart. He had fulfilled his heart's desire.

However, what Mustapha feared most finally came to pass. His father had used up the last strength he had to distribute the lands. When he heard the loud wail coming from his father's hut the next morning as dawn broke, he was broken. A deep sadness overtook him.

"Father!" he cried out, tears streaming down his cheeks. The mantle of leadership had now fallen on him.

The entire town attended the burial. Alhaji Suleiman had to be buried before the end of the day according to the Muslim tradition. His body was first cleansed in lukewarm water, and then wrapped. Janazah—a congregational prayer service took place. After the prayers, his remains wereburied.

His sons and grandsons cried out in sorrow as they bowed their heads: "He gave us his last gift."

After the period of mourning—which was ten days long—was over, the sons got up and reached for their farming tools to begin work immediately. They would start off on the uncultivated lands by felling down the trees. They would grow the business, expand their territory, and cause their father's name to remain relevant; spoken from the mouths of men in reverence, passed on from generation to generation.

With gusto, they marched to their different assigned portions. Abubakar, the fifth son of Alhaji Suleiman, and his four sons had the same spirit. They strutted to their land, men on a mission. Their farm hands were already present, awaiting them with the tractors and diggers.

Work began in earnest. When the first tree came down, there was a huge shout of celebration. Yes, the expansion had begun. They looked at each other, victory evident in their eyes. The world was there for the taking.

On the third day, they all set out for work. It wasn't noon yet, but the sun was high up in the clouds, and the scorching heat caused rivulets of sweat to trickle down their skin. The air was thick with the perpetual whiff of body odour, whilst an occasional breeze whipped across their nostrils. The constant clang of human voices and machinery coalesced into a cacophony of irritants that Abubakar felt he needed a breather from. His head was throbbing so much he had to get away for a bit. His sons were very capable.

Abubakar signaled to his first son, Ibrahim, who nodded at him in acknowledgement. He walked right into the copse of trees, straight into coolness, the trees acting as a sunblock against the scorching heat. As he walked farther, the noise abated, and his headache receded. He felt better, so he kept walking ahead. He hadn't come this far before. The branches slapped at him, leaving cuts and bruises on his exposed arms and face. He realised he needed to tread more carefully.

Hence, Abubakar came out of his self-indulgence, and began taking note of his surroundings and where he placed his feet. He had just gone a bit further when he stopped in his tracks.

What was he seeing?

He placed his hands over his eyes, looking for the invisible material that must have suddenly covered his eyes, making him see differently. When he brought his hands down, it was still there.

He walked to it on shaky legs, his mind trying to take in what he was seeing. Surely, it was alien to this terrain; certainly not what he had expected to find.

It was… It was a boulder, wasn't it?

Enormous and precariously balanced, the sight of it left Abubakar speechless.

How did this come about?

His father had owned these acres of land for years, and there had never been any mention of this. He couldn't comprehend this. Abubakar turned on his heels and ran back the way he had come, as fast as his legs could carry him. He needed to notify his sons and his brothers. This wasn't what they had expected to find.

CHAPTER THIRTEEN

Abubakar's sons couldn't make out what their father was trying to say. They stared at him strangely, their eyes darting back and forth, while Ibrahim edged closer, trying to examine him.

Abubakar looked exasperated. "Let's just go," he urged them forward, his heart still pounding at his discovery.

When his sons arrived at the spot, their backs ramrodded in shock, their mouths agape. The same question in their father's eyes mirrored in theirs. They were bolder, though. They crept closer, running their hands all over it.

"It's a rock," Ibrahim blurted out in amazement.

"It is!" the others agreed.

Ibrahim noticed a little piece of rock that had broken out from the boulder, lying a few metres away. He picked it up, running his hands over it. By this time, a crowd had gathered. Abubakar's workers had run as fast as they could, spreading the news to his brothers, who immediately came rushing down.

Ibrahim turned the rock around in his hands, staring at it in deep concentration. A loud gasp escaped his throat. There was a small area where the interior of the rock was visible. Ibrahim wiped the rock clean, his excitement mounting, while others looked on.

"What is happening?" Abubakar asked.

Ibrahim was too dumbfounded to speak. He tried to see beyond the outer layer of the rock. He thought he could see something; but he needed to be sure. "We need to go home!"

"I said, what is happening?" Abubakar asked again.

"Father, I don't know, but we need to find out."

Ibrahim trudged ahead with the others following behind. More family members joined at this point. Their loud banter preceded their appearance at the family compound. The women stood erect, bracing for the worst. Something must have happened for them to return this early. It had never happened before. It was almost noon, and they were just getting ready to deliver the already cooked porridge for the noon break.

Ibrahim requested for a penlight which one of the little children hurriedly brought to him. He shone the light against the rock surface but couldn't see well enough.

Abdul, his brother, produced a metal plate. Ibrahim had already figured the logic behind it. He placed it between his eyes and the penlight to eliminate any glare. As the light penetrated the rock, a smooth, verdant section glinted. He gasped. The rock fell down to his feet, his eyes bulging out of its socket.

"What is it?" they all asked at once.

"I saw something greenish inside!"

They took turns staring at it, wondering aloud what it was. Excitement buzzed in the air.

"We have to see Alhaji Sheriff immediately," Mustapha, the new patriarch of the family, announced. "He would know what it is."

Alhaji Sheriff was a collector of some sorts. He was now an old man, eighty-eight-years old, and bedridden by arthritis, but his wealth of knowledge was unchallenged. His place was a bit far. They had to leave immediately. Mustapha and the next nine sons behind him took off. The grandsons were anxious, curiosity lining their faces.

"We will be back soon," Mustapha said.

They walked in silence, but with hurried steps. An indescribable feeling coursed through Mustapha. He needed to know what the rock meant, but he didn't think he would like the outcome. He took a glance at his brothers and dread washed over him. *This rock wasn't good luck,* he thought. Their lives were about to change in ways he never imagined.

***

They got to Alhaji Sheriff's late in the evening, just before the sun began creeping back into the sky.

HajiaSadatu, his first wife, welcomed them.

"*Sannu dazuwa,*" she greeted.

"*Nagode,*" they thanked her.

She quickly served them water to drink to quench their thirst after the long journey. She came out a few minutes later, motioning them to remain where they sat.

Two sons of Alhaji Sheriff helped him out, his hands draped around their shoulders, as they placed him on the mat, with the wall of the house supporting his back. He was clearly happy to see them.

"*As-Salaam-Alaikum,*" they greeted him.

"*Wa-Alaikum-Salaam.* Please let's eat," he said.

His wives brought out the meal: *Tuwo Shinkafa*—a thick rice pudding with spicy sauce. They ate the meal in silence. When they were through, the wives cleared the dishes.

Alhaji Sheriff cleared his throat before he spoke. "To have ten sons of the great Alhaji Suleiman in my house is no easy feat. To what do I owe this?"

Mustapha summarised what had taken place that morning. He brought out the rock and presented it to Alhaji Sheriff.

Alhaji Sheriff took it from him and examined it for a bit, before asking one of his sons to bring him a penlight, a metal plate, and a small sharp knife. He repeated the same process that Ibrahim had applied with the penlight. The only emotion he showed was his brows furrowed in concentration. He used the sharp knife to cut a small part of the rock and cut a small hole in it. He polished the inside to see what lay beneath the surface. "You mean you saw this on the farm?"

"Yes," Mustapha said. "It was on Abubakar's portion of the farm."

Alhaji Sheriff dropped the rock on the ground. "I have seen things in this short life of mine," he began."But this seems to top it all. In the southern part of Kaduna, I have come in contact with gemstones like emerald and topaz. This rock came out of the ground just the way oil came out from the ground in the East. I don't know what it is. It is bigger than what I know. You may need to approach the authorities. It is most certainly a mineral resource."

On the way back home, Mustapha was in a pensive mood. Several thoughts whipped through his head. He wished his father, Alhaji Suleiman, was still alive. He would have known what to do. Mustapha didn't think he was strong enough to make decisions that would affect the lifestyle of the family. He just didn't have a good feeling about any of this.

When they arrived late at night, they wasted no time sitting down for a meeting with the Council of Elders. Late Alhaji Suleiman was the village headman, but upon his demise, it was passed on to his first son, Mustapha. The Council of Elders comprised seven elderly men whose advice was sought by the village headman and acted upon.

Mustapha stood up and in a few minutes explained what had happened. The rock was passed around for the Elders to see. The Elders were quiet for some time as they pondered the next step to take.

The first Elder spoke up: "We are farmers. The crops emerge from the soil and are a blessing to us. This rock has equally come out of the ground. I don't know if it is a blessing or a curse."

Another Elder picked up from where he stopped. "We may never know what this portends for us until we open up and let the authorities know."

The third Elder argued that point. "But what if it's a blessing? We would have let go of our secret and invited others in. Who knows, it may be a gift from the late Alhaji Suleiman. His spirit may have sent it to us," he added superstitiously.

It was the turn of the fifth Elder. "This is way beyond us. If there is more of that boulder present on the farm, we need to know. We don't even know what it is."

The sixth Elder continued: "We should remember that this land belongs to us. If this is a blessing, it must stay with us."

The seventh Elder disagreed. "We need information from those who know better than us, but we must be prepared to let go if it is way beyond us."

The seven Elders had spoken their minds. Mustapha, the village headman, got up and aired his view. "I think we should go to sleep with these thoughts. When we wake up in the morning, *In sha Allah*, we would be clear-minded and come to a decision."

They all agreed and stood up to disperse, their eyes heavy with worry, and their shoulders slumped with the weight of the decision they needed to make. Some stayed awake throughout the night, while others tossed and turned, their wives not able to render comfort to them. If they were aware of the events taking place behind the scene, they wouldn't have troubled their souls. Because come morning, their decisions made no difference. The situation had gone beyond them.

CHAPTER FOURTEEN

Sadiq was one of the workers of Abubakar on whose farmland they had found the boulder. He was present when the men trooped to the family compound and Ibrahim confirmed that there was something greenish inside the rock. He heard clearly when Mustapha decided that they should go to see Alhaji Sheriff. It meant that this was very important.

After they had dispersed, Sadiq rushed home to his father, Alhaji Abba, who was taking care of his animals. His father was into animal farming. Sadiq tried to catch his breath first before he launched into his story, watching his father's eyes grow wild like saucers.

Alhaji Abba pondered for a little while, pacing back and forth, before ambling to the back of the house where he splashed water on his face and washed his hands and feet. He stepped into the house and changed. At the door, he held his son by the shoulders, looked him in the eye, and said, "You have done well."

When Alhaji Abba walked into the office of Alhaji Ali, the new local government chairman, Alhaji Ali was just rounding off with his last visitor, who was stepping out.

Alhaji Ali was conversant with Alhaji Abba. He was one of the frequent visitors to his office, dropping bits of irrelevant information, wishing to ingratiate himself. At the sight of him so soon after the last visit, Alhaji Ali felt irritated. He wasn't in the mood for meaningless conversation. He was tired and needed to get home to relax and eat some food to assuage his hunger.

"Alhaji Abba," he began, a fake smile plastered on his face to his irritation. "I have just rounded off for today. Why don't you come first thing tomorrow morning?"

"No!" Alhaji Abba cried out, his hands in the air. "This is important. You have to hear this. The future of Doka is about to change and you must be informed!"

What was he talking about? Alhaji Ali wondered. Well, he would give him five minutes to say whatever it was so he could get a move on. He offered Alhaji Abba a seat.

Alhaji Ali's emotions went from wonder to incredulity to curiosity as Alhaji Abba divulged everything. He couldn't believe what he was hearing.

"Did you say on the farmland?"

"Yes!"

"And that they went to see Alhaji Sheriff?"

"Yes!"

This was serious. He needed to be on top of this and find out what was happening. According to the land use act, rural lands were under the care of the local government. He thanked Alhaji Abba for reporting promptly to him. His visit had yielded something productive for the first time. Alhaji Abba departed, looking pleased with himself. He had succeeded in ingratiating himself. Surely, he would be rewarded.

Alhaji Ali sat back in his office as he brooded on his next line of action. The Suleiman family were very well respected. In fact, he was present at the burial of their late father. Sending a representative would have been a slap in their face. He needed to tread softly with them; but he also needed to do his job. He was worried at their delay in not reporting their find immediately to his office. This could be the defining point in his political career. He picked up his phone and made a call.

***

The next morning, the twenty-five brothers were at home deliberating on what to do, having decided to not go to the farm that day until they had reached a decision. Unbeknownst to them, Alhaji Ali had arrived with Geo-scientists from the Geological Survey of Nigeria to look up the new find. Alhaji Abba was also present with his son to lead them to the spot. They were almost approaching the spot when the news got to Mustapha and his brothers.

The scientists stood in shock, taking in the sight, while the lead scientist, Dr. Tijani, picked up another piece of rock lying on the ground. He felt the need to return to his laboratory to examine it and find out what it was. It piqued his curiosity; his analytical mind already hyper-active.

They were making their way out of the copse of trees when Mustapha made his appearance with his twenty-four brothers, and their many grandsons. It was a sight to behold. They wore menacing looks and were visibly angry.

Mustapha spoke up. "You have no right to come here without our permission. This is our land."

Alhaji Ali knew that this was his first test. He needed to be polite, yet firm, passing his message across. "Mustapha, we are not here to pick a fight. The news got to me as it should, being the local government chairman. I am sure you are just as inquisitive as I am to know what this boulder is. These are Geo-scientists," he said, pointing at the people wearing white lab coats behind him. "They will take a sample of this rock to their laboratory and inform us of what it is. Please, let's all keep a cool head."

"But how did you get to know?" Mustapha pried.

One of his brothers pointed to Alhaji Abba and his son cowering behind the scientists.

"So, it's you," Abubakar gritted out. "You are betrayers. Traitors! I don't want to ever see you here again!"

"Please, just calm down," Alhaji Ali pleaded. "I will get in touch with you as soon as I receive word from the scientists."

The entire day at the office, Alhaji Ali couldn't think of anything else. When he got home, he opened up everything to his wife. They both waited in suspense for the call.

When the call came through late that evening, he jumped up, picking it off the cradle before the second ring. "Hello!"

"Hello, Alhaji Ali," Dr. Tijani replied, his words pouring out in an excited rush. "It is a Jade boulder. Jade is a precious gemstone and it consists of two minerals. The one present in this Jade is Jadeite. It is very rare and I must say one of the most valuable minerals in the world. Doka can never be the same again. I will come by your office tomorrow."

Doka had a mineral resource! A precious gem stone that was rare! Unbelievable!

At first light the next morning, Alhaji Ali left his house for the office.

***

Alhaja Amina went about her duties quickly so she could come see her friend. She had to share the news with her.

Later at Chinenye's shop, she allowed her fears to show.

"I am afraid for my husband. I wish he wasn't the chairman. You should have seen the fear on his face as he described what happened at the land yesterday when the twenty-five brothers confronted them. What do you think will happen now when they get to know that it is a very valuable mineral? They may refuse to let go of the land. I foresee violence, and my husband is in the thick of it."

"Don't worry," Chinenye said. "It would soon be off his hands. The federal government will come into the picture since mineral resources are vested with them. If they feel they are that strong, let them fight the federal government."

"I know that, but it still doesn't give me any modicum of peace. I don't like this at all. I don't," Alhaja Amina said. "I pray all this comes to an end pretty soon so we can get back to our lives."

She had spoken too quickly because the end she hoped for wasn't what played out.

***

In Grandma's room, they returned from their time travel to 1980. Grandma looked exhausted, but her eyes were alert.

Mr Julius broke the silence. "Grandma, I still cannot believe this. It's like the story of the Titanic, and the old woman who came out years later to describe the events that led to the sinking of the ship. I cannot thank you enough for making me a part of it.

Is it okay if I write all of this down? It only just occurred to me."

Grandma mulled over it for a few seconds. "Yes, you can do that. I don't think I may be able to repeat all of this a second time," she said, laughing lightly.

"Okay, Grandma. I would work with Gregory."

Gregory walked Mr Julius to the door. He sat down in the living room; the story riveting in his memory. He needed to hear more. He made a silent prayer to God to keep Grandma in good health and not allow her situation to worsen. She hadn't elapsed in the last few days. The sound of his mother's voice calling him brought him out of his reverie. He sprang to his feet.

CHAPTER FIFTEEN

Gregory had lost touch with 2015. He was presently living in the year 1980. Grandma's story was like a movie playing out in his head; only it had no end in sight yet. His friends harangued him, and he gave in, letting them in on the story. Mr Julius had warned him to keep the story a secret until they knew what to do with it. But he couldn't keep it away from his friends! They had played their part in getting Grandma to open up.

The downside of being so passionate was the commitment attached to it. Everything else suffered in the end. Gregory had lostinterest in his studies. He was too wrapped up with Jade.

He remained restless until Wednesday evening. They all congregated at his grandmother's room. Grandma's health had remained stable so far. Gregory was thankful to God. He couldn't imagine Grandma suffering a relapse, leaving part of the story untold. He was now addicted to Jade like a cocaine addict.

***

The once peaceful town of Doka had lost its calmness and serenity due to the discovery of Jade. The effect rippled all over the town as tension lingered in the atmosphere, gathering momentum and wrapping its inhabitants in it.

It was the talk of every home. Greed emanated from the eyes of husbands; anxiety flittered across the features of young men, and women pictured wealth and the new way of life associated with it. Different strings were being pulled in separate corners, and when they were all woven together, it resulted in a cataclysmic effect.

Mustapha's twenty-four brothers were beyond angry. The men of the household were in a meeting with the Council of Elders. Mustapha had already briefed the Elders on what had transpired. He had informed them through a letter earlier that morning that what was present in their farmland was a Jade boulder which contained Jadeite—a stone so rare and precious. Alhaji Sheriff, the collector, was also present to lend his advice. Soon, the conversation began.

The first Elder: "The deed has already been done, no thanks to the traitors. What I would like to know is what now becomes of the farmland?"

Alhaji Sheriff felt it expedient to speak. "According to the land use act, your land would automatically become a property of the federal government. But there will be compensation. They wouldn't take your land without requisite compensation."

A loud murmur of 'No!' 'Never' 'No one will take our land' filled his ears. When Alhaji Sheriff had mentioned compensation, Mustapha had felt relieved. The gemstone would be taken off of them and the compensation used to purchase new acres of land so they could go back to their normal way of life. Apparently, he had thought too soon. The reaction of his brothers and their sons filled him with dismay. He could see the hunger and desire in their eyes. They wanted the gemstone!

As the noise escalated, Mustapha sat down, confused on what step to take. He wished again that their father had not passed away at such a critical time when he was needed most.

***

Alhaji Ali sat in his office, deep in thought. He had earlier refused all calls and visits for the day so he could have sufficient time to think properly and come up with his next line of action. He knew that the right thing to do was to pick up his phone and call the Governor of the state to inform him of his find, so it could be passed on to the federal government.

But something held him back.That something that caused God to look down upon mankind and feel regret over ever creating them; expressly stating that the heart of man is wicked.

Alhaji Ali needed to find a way to exploit the situation to his benefit. He had the lead scientist and his team wrapped around his thumb. They wouldn't give his secret away. This was a rare gemstone.

Couldn't he find a way to get around this?

Mustapha and his brothers faced him on one side; his duties on the other. Suddenly, a snap decision came through him. He picked up his phone.

***

In a secluded hotel owned by a wealthy businessman in Kaduna, a group of men, numbering twenty, were seated on chairs made of ivory, arranged around a large table in a basement below the hotel that was unknown to the public and some of its staff.

The men wore pensive, hard looks. They were a diverse mixture of aristocrats, civil servants, cabinet members, businessmen, intellectuals, bank managers, and military colonels. They held positions of power; known for their intelligence, commitment to traditional values, and socio-political interests in northern Nigeria. They had used their alliance with the presidency to obtain patronage and disburse favour to friends and associates. They were known as the 'Kaduna Mafia'.

A civil servant kicked off the conversation. He was a top civil servant in one of the ministries. "This news portends a lot for Kaduna; and for the North. It completely changes the dynamics."

A bank manager picked up from where he stopped. "We have been occupied today, flooded with visits requesting for loans. People are already seeking capital just at the mention of Jade without even seeing it. It is already causing a frenzy. As an organisation, we are prepared to collaborate with the federal government."

A businessman with a large investment in the transportation business added his bit. "I am already looking into purchasing excavators and other equipment that would be needed. I am eyeing being an independent contractor."

It was the turn of a cabinet member. "I wonder why Alhaji Ali is yet to make an official declaration. It would be stupid of him to not realise that we would be in the know by now."

A lecturer from one of the prestigious universities in the North chipped in: "What does this portend for the political structure. Remember, it's the interest of northern Nigeria first above our interests. The country has just survived a civil war, but the peace is still very fragile. The voices of the agitators haven't been totally silenced. We have been successful in the domination of oil from the East. How would other regions receive the news of the presence of our own mineral resource?"

A military colonel got up in a huff, angry veins sticking out on his forehead. "They can receive it however they please. May I refresh your memory in case this important piece of information has been relegated to the background that they started the civil war when they assassinated the Sultan of Sokoto, Sir Ahmadu Bello, in an Igbo military coup in January 1966? They can secede for all I care. Allah has blessed us with a gift: Jade. If they want war, we will give them war!"

The looks on the faces of others mirrored his. Yes, the country could be divided. They had their own resources. All they wanted was the progress of northern Nigeria. They had been blessed with a gift to make it work. Allah be praised!

***

Across the River Niger, a similar meeting was taking place in Onitsha. The Obi of Onitsha, Igwe Nwankwor Okoye, was seated upon his throne, in his palace, dressed in his regalia: a crown atop his head decorated with various feathers, a white gown which covered his body; from his head to his toes, beaded bracelets on his wrists, a beaded necklace around his neck and his hand, and his bronze staff in his hand; surrounded by his red-cap chiefs known as 'Ndichie Ume'. They were the most powerful and senior members of the Obi's inner circle. They were six in number: Onowu—likened to the prime minister, Ajie, Odu, Onya, Ogene, and Owelle.

"Is it true?" the Obi asked, anxiously.

"Yes, it is true, your highness," the Onowu said. "We have received three messages from our men in Doka. They have 'Jade'."

The Obi's voice boomed out after a few seconds of contemplation. "Send messages across immediately. Everybody needs to be aware."

The Chiefs got up to do his bidding.

***

Alhaji Ali could rest easy for a bit. He had no choice but to inform the Governor's office. This was a sensitive situation. He needed to be in the clear. It wouldn't have augured well for him if they had found out from a different source.

Next, he had concluded arrangements to buy excavators to begin the process of mining as soon as the paperwork was ready to be presented to Mustapha and his brothers. Since he was down here, and close to home, he was in the thick of it, and would remain on top of the situation. He wouldn't allow himself to be outsmarted. He could already visualise the riches just within his reach. A wicked smile spread across his face.

***

In her shop, Chinenye was seated with Alhaja Amina. She had never seen her friend looking this distraught. It was as if an assailant had taken a knife to her neck. She could barely complete a sentence. Her teeth clattered in fear.

"This Jade would be the death of us, Chinenye. I can feel it. It isn't a blessing. It's a curse. Why did my husband have to be in the position of power now, eh? I am afraid of Mustapha and his brothers. News travelling around says that Mustapha cannot even keep a handle on their temper. They could harm my husband. My joy at his appointment has turned to sorrow," she cried out, worried lines etched so deeply across her forehead.

Chinenye felt so bad seeing her this way. Her vivacious, delightful friend was gone and now replaced with this fearful, worried person. The light had gone out of her eyes. She couldn't bear to see her this way. She had to make her return to her normal self, although she realised it would be a daunting task.

"You cannot continue this way," Chinenye pleaded. "You have to overcome your fears. Your daughter, Hadiza, will be back from London in three days after a grueling time pursuing her degree. How would she feel seeing you like this? Things may turn out well in the end, eh!"

"Hadiza!" she whispered painfully. "How I wish she would remain where she is. But she is stubborn and wishes to return home as soon as possible. She wouldn't listen to me. She would be safe there."

"Oh, stop it! Please, just stop it! Nothing bad is going to happen. You need to stop this. Look at my daughter, Ngozi. Can't you see her crying? You are frightening her with your look."

Ngozi had begun crying because her three-year-old mind couldn't process what was happening.

"I am sorry, Chinenye," Alhaja Amina said, scurrying out of the shop.

CHAPTER SIXTEEN

It was formerly known as the Lagos International Airport. The new airport terminal, however, was renamed for the late Nigerian Head of State, General Murtala Muhammed, who died in 1976, and was opened officially March 15, 1979. The plane landed at the Murtala Muhammed International Airport, just as the early morning light began to rear its head. Hadiza had slept through the entire trip and was glad to be waking up on another continent.

She climbed down the staircase onto the tarmac, breathing in the Nigerian air, which brought back sweet memories of home. She quickly blinked back the tears that threatened to spill down her cheeks. Through the customs and immigration checks, she was fidgety. She couldn't wait to see her mother's face. When she eventually came into the arrival hall, her frantic eyes scanned the crowd.

Suddenly, she was pulled into a hug so tight she could scarcely breathe. When she finally disentangled from the hug, she stared right into the face of her mother's cousin, Alhaja Latifat. She peered behind her aunty, searching. Her smile faltered.

Alhaja sensed her disappointment. "Your mother couldn't be here. Let's step out of here, and I will explain better."

Hadiza picked up her suitcases from the baggage carousel, trailing her aunty behind. On the way to her aunt's place at Festac, Aunty Alhaja filled her in on the developments at Doka. To say she was disappointed was an understatement. Her father had passed a stern warning that she couldn't come down to Doka until it was considered safe.

How absurd was that?

She had encountered all manner of challenges living abroad as a young African woman. She had survived the odds, and graduated with a degree in communications, only for her to return to her country and be barred from seeing her parents, because it wasn't safe! *Home was supposed to be a safe haven, wasn't it?*

This definitely wasn't the homecoming she had envisaged. Her mother couldn't even come to see her until a few weeks later. She wondered how she would pass the time. Her aunty's sons were eight and ten respectively; not a suitable company for a twenty-three-year-old.

As the car drove through the main gate, making a stop at the car park, Hadiza was already busy recalling the names of friends she had in Lagos whom she could call upon. She only hoped that they were available.

***

Three days later, Hadiza lay sprawled on the couch in her room, bored. She needed to get out or she would lose her mind. It was time to make those calls. She picked up her phone and began thumbing through the contacts. When she came upon Fatima's number, she tapped it and watched it dialing. Fatima picked up on the third ring, to the delight of Hadiza.

By six o'clock in the evening, Hadiza sauntered into the spacious living room in Fatima's house. A throng of young men and women were scattered about, dressed to the nines. She sighted Fatima standing by a corner of the room with a man and two women. She made her way towards her, picking up a cocktail drink from the tray of a passing waiter. Fatima looked in her direction at that moment.

"Hadiza!" she exclaimed, scurrying to meet Hadiza half-way as they murmured greetings to each other, carefully air-kissing each other's cheeks.

"Happy Birthday, Fatima!" Hadiza said. "I am so glad I called you today, or I would have missed this. Please, take this," she added, pushing a gift wrapped in shiny sheets towards Fatima.

"Thank you, Hadiza. Please make yourself comfortable. The buffet table is at the end of the room." Fatima pointed at a table filled with several food trays before she walked away to welcome another set of visitors who had just trooped in.

Hadiza took in the room. She couldn't recognise any familiar face amongst the crowd. According to Fatima, it was meant to be a low key party, but the place was almost filled up. The chairs had been dragged to the corners, freeing up space for movements. A lovely display of several colours of light filtered across the room and soft music played from hidden speakers.

Hadiza found a spot on the right that had just been vacated. She slipped into the seat, moving her body to the rhythm of the music, tapping her feet to the song. A few minutes later, Hadiza's hand trembled as she held the glass. She had felt weird; like she was being watched. She scanned the room, her eyes darting back and forth.

Soon, she found the looker.

He had cast his eyes away, but not fast enough. He was by the buffet table, serving himself. She peered at him; her pupils pinpoints of concentration. She could swear that she didn't know him. The looker glanced in her direction again. When he caught her gaze on him, he grinned, revealing a beautiful white set of teeth.

He began walking towards her.

Hadiza noted his well-built body, wide set of shoulders, and easy gait. His face wasn't classically handsome, but rather, filled with character so intense it drew her in. So drawn she didn't realise he had been standing in front of her.

"A penny for your thoughts," he said, breaking the spell, flashing a smile that showed his pearly-white teeth again.

There wasn't anything to say. She had been caught. Hadiza giggled to hide her embarrassment.

"I am Clement Okoye," he said.

"I am Hadiza Muhammed."

They shook hands, their gazes lingering on each other far longer than the handshake.

"Please, join me," Clement offered, tipping his plate filled with small chops towards her. Hadiza loved small chops. She picked up a toothpick, sinking it into a samosa.

***

By the time the party was over, they both knew that friendship wouldn't suffice. When Clement had first laid his eyes on Hadiza as she stepped into the room, he had known in that special way that men always know; that Hadiza was the woman for him.

They spent two weeks enjoying each other's company. They attended parties together; walked hand in hand by the beach, ate roasted corn and coconut by the roadside, and watched movies together. In fact, they were hardly out of each other's company.

After another time out at the beach two Saturdays after, they both sat down on the sand, watching the waves roll over, crashing onto each other.

"You know we are both like these waves. We are intertwined," Clement said, facing her. He expected to see a happy face, but a line of worry that quickly vanished off her face troubled him. "What is it, my love?"

"My aunty is already asking questions. She says a responsible girl shouldn't be out this much with someone who isn't her husband."

"Is that it?" Clement laughed. "But that is not a problem! I want to marry you. Don't you know that there is no other woman for me?"

Hadiza kept mute.

"What is it, Hadiza? Come on, talk to me."

"Are you serious about marrying me?"

"Yes, I am."

"But you know it cannot be," she choked out, dragging the words.

"What do you mean? So what have we been doing? Playing?"

"Clement, look around you. Can't you see what is happening in our country? The hatred is so apparent."

"Why are you talking like this? We are exposed and educated. Let's talk to our parents. We are not part of this hatred. We will be a beacon of light shining through for people to see that love dwells everywhere, irrespective of tribal, religious, or social status differences. I was going to tell you that I would be travelling next week to see my father. I will bring this up when I get there."

"Clement, your father is the Obi of Onitsha. What makes you think he will accept this? He will expect you to marry an Igbo girl."

"I would not marry an Igbo girl," Clement said stubbornly. "He asked for me. He says it's urgent. I will go to him immediately and discuss this with him. Please, have faith in me."

"I am equally worried about my parents. I think I will go see them without informing them of my arrival. I worry more after every phone conversation with my mother. She sounds very distant and disturbed. I know that my father's appointment as the local government chairman would keep them on their toes, especially with the discovery of Jade, but I don't like the sound of my mother's voice. I am an only child. I should be by their side. I want to go and see them."

"I will help you with the travel arrangements. While you are there, you can tell your parents about us, because believe it or not, I am coming with my people to ask for your hand in marriage."

They hugged. Clement held her tight, his arms wrapped around her in a protective embrace. He was her protector. He would protect this relationship from all the odds stacked against it. This was his solemn vow.

***

Back in Grandma's room, Gregory could see the strain telling on Grandma's face. Even Mr Julius looked concerned.

Outside the door, he voiced his concerns. "I think we need to let her rest for a while. It can't be easy recalling all these events. Let's give her some space."

As much as Gregory felt the same, time wasn't on their side. Yes, they would give her time to recover, but he just hoped that she wouldn't suffer a relapse, or have her condition deteriorate further. They were basically walking on pins and needles.

CHAPTER SEVENTEEN

The next morning, it happened again. Gregory woke up to loud voices. He bounced off the bed and rushed out of his room towards the noise. He peered into his grandmother's room, his mouth agape. His mother was struggling with his grandmother, who was trying to get up from the chair. He must have made a sound because his mother turned to him and shouted, "Gregory, come and help me!"

Gregory had no idea it would be so difficult for two people to keep her still.

"Who are you people? I don't know you. You must be kidnappers! Let me go!" Grandma screamed until she exhausted herself and kept still.

For the first time, Gregory was late to school. The school hours went by in a haze. By the time he returned home, things were quieter. The violence and fighting had ceased. Gregory had a bite mark from the scuffle that morning. It was difficult to comprehend that a woman, who had spoken so clearly yesterday, in twenty four hours, could become disoriented and confused.

By that evening, Gregory was now Chijioke, Grandma's late husband, while ironically, his mother was now Alhaja Amina. The only problem was that this wasn't her house. She wanted to go to her house;

this she kept repeating. They had to play the part. That was the only way she let them get close to her.

Gregory stepped into his room, angry and hurt. He was angry at the disease called 'Alzheimer's' which could so rudely strip away a person's memory and coordination, leaving behind a veneer of decay and disruption. Grandma had started first by forgetting things and then recalling later. But now, it was much worse. It hurt him seeing her this way; the light in her eyes gone, leaving a cold indifference and aloofness. The tears streamed down his eyes, and he cried till he couldn't shed any more tears.

The next day at school, he informed Mr Julius of the deteriorating situation.

"It's okay, Gregory. She will come off it. Remember, you said it is at stage four. I read up on it, too. It will take a while to proceed to the next stage."

"What if she gets worse and doesn't recover?"

Mr Julius refused to allow his opinion be swayed. "Let's just watch and see how it pans out. Your grandmother is a strong woman."

Gregory watched the days go by, his grandmother still in her state of disorientation. He wasn't faring better either. He had lost appetite for food and lost interest in his studies. His marks would have declined but for the aid of his friends who helped with his assignments. Thankfully, there were no more unprepared tests in class.

His friends tried to cheer him up. Even the entire class joined in, but it was to no avail. By the second week, Gregory had lost hope. His grandmother was lost to him. The story of Jade never to be completed. Even Mr Julius' optimism suffered, too. He carried himself lethargically, like the walking dead. Each day after the morning assembly, he would walk up to Gregory to ask, "Is she better?"

This was what Jade had done to them. They were a shadow of their former selves. Jade had reached out to them in 2015 to turn their lives into chaos. Its power was never ending; its grip tight, with a self-inflicting injury of unrestrained agony.

The weekend was uneventful. Gregory spent the entire time in his room. He couldn't bear to walk past his grandmother's room and see her staring at the ceiling, dazed, or working herself up in an argument with his mother, who wore a forlorn look as she watched over her. He summoned all the energy he possessed to walk with his friends to school the following Monday, sitting through classes absentmindedly. School was now torture. When the bell went off for the closing assembly, he went through the process mechanically. He didn't know which was worse: staying at school or returning home.

He walked into the living room, dragging his footsteps, only to see his mother standing, smiling.

That was funny.

There had been no smiles and laughter in the house for more than two weeks. He looked at her morosely.

"Your Grandma wants to see you."

Gregory couldn't! He couldn't dare to believe. He was afraid to do so.

"Go on," his mother urged.

He dropped his school bag on the floor and ran to his grandma's room.

Grandma looked in his direction at the sound of the door opening. "Greg, how was school today?"

He couldn't answer. The sweet appellation 'Greg' was too much for him to take. He pushed himself forward, encircling her in an embrace. They held onto each other, crying and sniffing loudly. His mother had come to the door, crying too. It was a happy reunion.

His mother warned him not to bring up the topic of Jade. Gregory was happy to oblige. Having Grandma back was more than enough even though he didn't know how long it would last. She recognised them today. Let them at least enjoy it.

Mr Julius was overjoyed to hear the news the next day. The entire class celebrated during lunch break. She had become everyone's grandmother. Her pain and joy were theirs to share, too.

In the days that followed, Gregory and his mother treaded softly, trying not to do anything to agitate Grandma and trigger her mood swing. They were just happy to have her back. Her life was more important than a story. Gregory was content.

That weekend, he kept his grandma company in her room. They watched a comedy show and laughed so hard their sides hurt. When the program ended, Gregory got up to slot in another compact disc.

"Greg, how about that teacher of yours?"

Gregory turned around, stunned. His answer came out in a stammer. "He is fine, Grandma."

"When is he going to come around? We have unfinished business."

His mother heard that last statement as she walked in. "*Nne*, are you sure you are ready for this?"

"Yes, I am," Grandma said.

In school the next day, Gregory almost knocked Mr Julius down when he ran into him. "Grandma wants to see you," he blurted out. "She is ready to finish it up."

Mr Julius' eyes shone in wonder. "Are you sure?"

"Yes," he said, breathless. "She asked after you yesterday."

"I am so elated to hear that, Gregory. Your grandma is one tough woman. Let's meet up after school."

They were huddled on the bed, biting into the carton of cupcakes that Mr Julius brought who knew he had a soft side—as Grandma picked up from where she stopped.

***

In Doka, Alhaji Ali was staring intently at the papers in front of him. The previous week he had received news from the geo-scientists of the discovery of a second Jade boulder on Abubakar's land. The papers before him were from the federal government en route to the governor's office, directing him to ascertain the true value of the lands for due compensation to be handed to the family so the mining process could begin.

The situation was becoming trickier and more complicated, but he wouldn't be thrown into a corner. He would remain on top of this. He began the process of forwarding the papers to Mustapha and his brothers.

***

The men were seated across the large table once more, their faces more agitated.

The cabinet member spoke up. "Mustapha and his brothers should be taking delivery of the papers by now. All has been set in motion."

The lecturer added, "It is time for northern Nigeria to rise and take its place. We are prepared."

The military colonel cut in."My men are ready to swing into action as soon as I pass on my orders. Coded messages have been sent to other northern states. It has been received well. We are all on the same track."

The last piece of news from the colonel was all they needed to hear. There was no turning back now.

***

In late Alhaji Suleiman's compound, Mustapha was in a meeting with the Council of Elders and his brothers. The mood was leaning towards violence. The papers had been received and read out for all to hear.

Mustapha spoke up. "My brothers, they are ready to compensate. Let us accept this money and buy land elsewhere."

"No!" his brothers answered in unison.

"It is our land! We should be allowed to do what we want with it," Abubakar declared.

"But we wouldn't be at a loss. We would be compensated," Mustapha pointed out.

"We don't need their compensation. Our late father gave us this land. It is ours by right," Abubakar asserted.

Mustapha was too exasperated to throw in a counter line of argument.

An Elder raised his voice above the melee. "You are missing the point. Your father preached peace. This attitude you are all putting up will lead to bloodshed. You can't fight the government. Listen to us and your brother, who is the patriarch o your family and the present village headman. Let this go!"

"No!" Abubakar roared back. "He is no patriarch. He is so lily-livered. He has vehemently refused to fight for what is ours. We would not let our father down. We wouldn't surrender!"

With that, the twenty-four brothers stormed out of the meeting, leaving Mustapha nonplussed. His position as first son had just been usurped by Abubakar, the fifth son.

CHAPTER EIGHTEEN

In the palace of the Obi of Onitsha, Igwe Nwankwor Okoye, was seated on his throne, surrounded by his chiefs, and representatives from the Dein of Agbor and the other oil producing states, which were, Ondo, Rivers, and Cross River.

The Onowu started off the conversation. "From the reports received from our trusted spy, the North are almost ready to begin the mining of Jade."

The Ogene: "The military are secretly getting ready. Other northern states are in on this and are in support of the motion of division. The Kaduna mafia have pulled up all the stops."

The representative from the Dein of Agbor shared his view. "The message is clear. We no longer have a country. They have used this so-called democracy to their advantage; enriching themselves. Now, they want out."

The Obi cleared his throat before speaking. "Then so shall it be. I will not allow my people to be sidelined once again. You all know what to do. Let them become aware that we know; and if it is separation they want; we are ready to secede. Also, let it be known that they have no business with our oil. It is ours. We will protect it with our lives."

The men stood up; the meeting closed. Before the day ended, messages had been passed on. The groups that had been quiet since the end of the civil war suddenly found their voice again. What was thought a secret in the North had now become widespread!

When Clement sat down that evening with his father, the enormity of the situation hit him. This was bigger than he thought. His voice came out as a squeak as he tried to reason with his father. "But Father, we can't be plunged into another civil war. We are still smarting from the previous one. Can't this situation be managed?"

The Obi turned to his son. "I wish it were so, but it has gone beyond that. They are ready to move on, and so would we. This time we would stand tall. The crux of this matter is that there is no love amongst us."

Clement sprang to his feet, his voice raised. "There is love, Igwe. I know this because I have felt it."

The Obi's brows furrowed in annoyance. "Felt what, my son? What are you talking about?"

Clement realised this was the opportunity he needed. "I love a woman. Her name is Hadiza. She is from Doka in Kaduna, but she is…"

"She is what?" The Obi cut him off, his eyes bulging out of its sockets. "A Hausa woman! From the same Doka where this issue is springing from! Are you out of your senses?"

Clement's mother rushed in, taking in the situation with a glance. "What is happening, Igwe? *Ogini?* The sound of your voice is resounding all over the palace."

The Obi pointed at Clement. "Talk to your son. What he has said is impossible. I believe he said it in a moment of madness. I don't want to hear of this in my palace ever again," he warned as he stormed out.

Lolo Chizoba was in a quagmire. "What is he talking about, Clement? What is wrong?"

Clement couldn't believe what had just taken place. Surely, his mother would understand. "Mum, you have to talk to Dad. I am old enough to decide for myself."

"Sit down, my son. Tell me all."

***

The shrill sound of the phone ringing permeated the silence of the room. A hand shot out to pick it up from its cradle.

"Hello," the voice greeted, laced with a northern accent.

"Hello, my friend," the voice on the other end replied, resonant with the accent of the easterners. They had resolved to never use their names when talking on the phone.

"Is everything going as planned?" the northern voice asked.

"Yes, all is well here. Is your own part covered?"

"Not yet! There are still some loose knots that need to be tied up. It isn't as easy as it seems."

The voice on the other end let out a deep sigh. "We have to be on top of this. Our interests must be protected."

"It will be, my friend! Patience is all I ask for. Remember, a patient dog eats the fattest bone."

That put the easterner at ease. "All right, my friend. Let's talk again at the affixed time."

***

Chinenye couldn't be placated. Her father-in-law had passed on in her arms the previous night. The death of his wife had left a toll on him, which he never recovered from. Just like his wife, he would be buried in Kaduna. Alhaja Amina was there for the burial to console her and her husband, alongside customers from the shop. Even in the midst of several easterners, Alhaja Amina was comfortable.

After the crowd had dispersed, they both sat down on a long bench in front of her mud house. Ngozi, now a three-year-old, was playing with kids her age. Worry laced Alhaja Amina's face. Chinenye had gotten used to seeing her this way. Now all that Alhaja Amina did was lament and complain. She couldn't afford to tell her that she was weighed down with her complaints.

Alhaja Amina soon began. "It's been six months since the discovery of Jade, Chinenye. Mustapha's brothers have refused to stand down. Why couldn't they just be as peace-loving as the first son, Mustapha?"

"Don't worry. All this will pass soon," Chinenye assured her.

"When would it be, Chinenye? I don't know my husband anymore. He changed. This 'Jade' has possessed him completely. I fear he might do something irrational soon. He is like a ticking time bomb. I fear if I leave him for a minute, he would lose his senses. I have been unable to see my daughter since she returned from London five months ago, but I can't let her come here either. The situation is so tense. Now, I don't even know who is giving me a greater headache between my husband and daughter."

Chinenye picked up on that. "Ah! Is Hadiza giving you any problem?"

"Why do I have to be plagued with these problems? I just want peace. Why couldn't Hadiza just pick a Hausa boy, eh?"

"What are you saying?" she pressed on.

"That is the reason I refused her coming when my cousin, Alhaja Latifat, intimated me of what was happening and her desire to surprise us with a visit. She overheard Hadiza on the phone concluding arrangements with the boy. Hadiza has fallen in love with an Igbo boy and says she must marry him."

"When did this happen?"

"She met him at a party in Lagos. What is worse is that my husband overheard the conversation on the phone with my cousin. He blew hot and gave Hadiza an ultimatum. She must not return until she has parted ways with the boy. What is most troubling is that he is the son of the Obi of Onitsha. According to Hadiza, he is equally facing problems getting his father to accept her, too. Hadiza is stubborn. She has refused to let go. What should I do? My family is slipping away."

Chinenye held her close. They stared into nothingness until darkness descended. Alhaja Amina wished for the year to roll to an end and another to begin. Perhaps things would change and everything would get better, she desperately hoped.

CHAPTER NINETEEN

A year later.

In the basement, underneath the secluded hotel, the atmosphere had never been this tense. The mood was bordering on violence. It was in the air. They could smell it.

The military colonel smacked his palm hard on the table in anger, jolting everyone. "This has gone on for far too long. A single family can't hold back the progress of northern Nigeria."

The lecturer tried to calm the situation. "I understand where they are coming from. We need to take it easy with them."

"Take what easy?" the minister snarled. "Do you know the level of economic gains we would have made by now? This is almost the end of 1981. They have held us to ransom for a year!"

"Do you know we are being laughed at by the easterners? They say we possess no guts like them; and that we are lily-livered and all mouth," the businessman chipped in.

The military colonel jumped to his feet. "We will show them. If no one is ready to take on Mustapha and his brothers; I will."

"What will you do?" the lecturer asked, dreading the answer.

"What I need to do for the progress of northern Nigeria. I just never imagined that I would do this against my own brothers."

The message in his words sank into their minds. No one opposed. It had to be done.

***

The phone rang and was picked up immediately.

"What is happening?" the eastern voice questioned. "It's hard to believe that a year has passed and we aren't making any tangible headway. We are losing money."

"I have always told you to be patient," the northern voice said.

"For god's sake, my name is not patience! I am a businessman. I look for opportunities and sink my teeth into it. I thought you were the right man."

For the first time, there was anger in the voice of the northerner. "And what do you mean by that? Do not insult me. If you can't have patience, then let's end this now!"

The easterner was angry, but the threat in the statement pierced through his thoughts. "Haba, my friend! It's not so. I am just fed up with things being at a standstill."

"It wouldn't be anymore."

"What? Is something going on there?"

"Yes! If you had let me speak instead of haranguing me the way you did, you would have known already. Things are moving forward. We would soon smile. Remember the patient dog…"

"… Eats the fattest bone!" the eastern voice joined in with a loud chuckle. "I am happy now. I would be expecting your call."

The call ended.

***

Alhaji Ali seethed with so much rage, he saw red. He couldn't sit still. He pranced back and forth across his office. "Damn, these brothers!"

They had refused to surrender their land. The Geo-scientists had steered clear of the land for a while now. Even after the compensation increased, they bluntly refused. He knew Mustapha was now a figurehead, but he couldn't control his brothers. Did the twenty-four brothers believe they were stronger than the government?

The government was trying to do things right; but where had it gotten them so far? Why was the government cowering in a corner like a chicken soaked by the rain? If they couldn't do anything, then what could he do?

No, wait, why couldn't he?

This was his domain. Alhaji Ali had power here. He would show them what he was capable of doing. He had been patient enough. It was time to take action. He picked up the phone on his table and dialed a number. The redness in his line of sight had disappeared.

***

Hadiza lay wrapped in Clement's arms. They were at their favourite spot—the beach. They had been this way in companionable silence for a length of time.

Clement broke the silence. "We can't go on this way. I don't think this division that is bandied about would take place. The various groups clamouring for division have grown quiet in the last few months. I need to revisit the issue of our marriage with my father. I still can't believe that you haven't seen your parents yet. Aren't they tired of the phone calls? Can't your father change his stance?"

"I don't think this is the right time to discuss this."

"What do you mean, Hadiza? Sometimes, I think you do not want this relationship to grow beyond where it is at the moment. Any time I bring up the topic of how this relationship should move forward, you always have something negative to say. You say you love me; yet you don't want to fight for us. I don't understand you," Clement said.

Hadiza's eyes glistened with pain as she sat up. "I am going to forgive you for saying these things. I don't think I would have stayed with you if I didn't love you. I may not possess the same courage as you, but that doesn't mean I don't value what we share. Things may be quiet now, but it isn't over. My aunty discovered my plans to travel last year and gave me away. I will try to be careful this time. In fact, I am resolute. I have to go see my parents. There is this unsettling feeling of dread that has been hovering over me for days. It has upturned my mood."

Clement sighed. "I am telling you, my love, that this will pass. I wish I could go with you to see your parents, at least to protect you. I'm very sure that by the time you get there, you will see that your fears are unfounded. Make sure you bring up the issue about us when you are there. When you talk with them face-to-face, they would give in. That is the only reason I am letting you go."

"What?" Hadiza let out in playful shock. "Do I have to take permission from you before I go anywhere?"

"Of course! I am your husband," he huffed, pushing his chest forward.

Hadiza couldn't help laughing. "Not yet!"

"You will see," he teased, touching the tip of her nose. "Let's get ready for your trip. When do you want to leave?"

"In two days. I just feel the need to see them as soon as possible. My father has kept me away for far too long. I am ready to face the consequences when I get there."

"Okay, my princess. Let's make it happen."

***

In the palace of the Obi of Onitsha, the Igwe was in a meeting with his chiefs.

"Our spy confirms that things may begin to be set in motion in the North, Igwe," the Owelle said.

"I had begun to wonder if the Jade had disappeared, hence the prolonged silence," the Ajie said.

"They may not have taken any major step with the Jade yet; but that hasn't stopped them from reaping benefits from our oil, all to our detriment," the Ogene added.

"This democracy is a farce! A scam! Serving one region to the deterioration of others. There is no equity," the Onya said.

"Do we need equity? If we have to go our separate ways so we can live in peace, rule over what we have, and see socio-economic growth in our land, then let it be. We didn't get involved in the civil war for no reason," the Onowu declared.

It was time for the Igwe to speak. "These are trying times. Our ancestors fought and died for a country that doesn't want to see us live in unity. It is tragic. Only time will tell how things will pan out. In the interim; keep your ears to the ground. We must not be caught unawares."

"Igwe!" they all chanted in unison.

CHAPTER TWENTY

Several households woke up to the start of a normal day. Husbands proceeded to their places of work, shops, and farms. Wives headed to the market to begin the day's sales. Children weren't left out, as they either flocked to their schools, or went about their duties.

As for those who had no reason to leave the confines of their homes, they lay sprawled on mats outside their homes or engaged in other activities to pass the time. When the sun rose high in the sky, throwing its heat downwards, many were fast asleep; unaware of the big flies hovering and perching on them.

In that place of unconsciousness, they had their blissful sleep abruptly cut off by a loud, shrill sound in the distance. It permeated their sleep, disrupting it, as they got up angrily to investigate the reason for the noise.

Soon, a crowd of people gathered on the streets, perplexed by the sight of the long line of cars filled with police escorts, wearing menacing looks, gripping their rifles tight, with trucks carrying heavy equipment following closely behind.

It was after the cars had sped fast that an old man spoke up: "Was it not the car of the chairman that was second in line?"

The long file of cars soon reached its destination: Abubakar's land. Abubakar's workers had cut the trees down, so it was easy for them to drive to the spot. Alhaji Ali came down from his vehicle, flanked by two escorts, as the excavators were being prepared to do their job.

The excavators would extract the Jade from the ground, which was exposed using diamond-tipped core drills in order to extract samples. Then, the hydraulic spreaders would be inserted into cleavage points in the rock so the Jade could be broken away.

The process was already far gone when Mustapha and his twenty-four brothers got wind of what was taking place on their land. Hot anger coursed through their veins as they rallied around, grabbing cutlasses, shovels, and whatever weapon they could lay their hands on.

"What are you all doing?" Mustapha cried out. "They have got guns. You wouldn't stand a chance."

His words fell on deaf ears. The twenty-four sons and their grandsons, who were old enough to fight, ran out of the compound, poised for war.

***

Alhaji Ali watched the entire process taking place. "Can't it go faster?"

Dr. Tijani spoke sharply to his colleagues. Alhaji Ali beamed with satisfaction as he watched them speed up the process. The Jade would soon be in his possession.

Just then, the gunshots rang out. He knew it!

"Hurry up! Be quick!" he urged the scientists. "Get whatever you can."

A policeman rushed to him, breathless. "They are almost upon us. They are chanting and brandishing farm tools!"

"Don't let them get near here until I am ready to leave," he instructed.

The acrid smell of the gunshots permeated the air, and the screams of men rose alongside the clash of metal against metal. The scientists had abandoned the quest to lift the boulder. They were instead drilling holes into it, breaking it into pieces they could leave with.

Alhaji Ali was sweating profusely. The fight was escalating. More men had left him to join others fighting at the front.

"It's enough," he shouted. "Put those pieces in the car, and let's go."

"What of the others in front?" Dr. Tijani asked.

The question was received with silence. They got into the cars, as all the pieces were put in Alhaji Ali's car. As they began edging out, Dr. Tijani let out a frightened gasp. Men lay sprawled on the ground, moaning in pain and badly injured, while many others lay stiff and lifeless. Blood smeared the land, the smell thick in the air.

Dr. Tijani felt ashamed to see that most of the dead were the sons of late Alhaji Suleiman. They didn't stand a chance. A few had retreated, running back the way they had come. At that point, he felt sorry for what they had done. This is what greed had led them to. He turned to express his remorse to Alhaji Ali and find a way out before it was too late, but stopped in his tracks. He was staring into the eyes of a madman.

Just what had he gotten himself into?

***

Chinenye was in her shop when one of the young girls who lived with Alhaja Amina ran into the shop.

"Please, come ma!" the girl begged. "My madam wants to see you."

She got up, alarmed. What could have stopped her friend from coming to the shop?

Was she sick?

She quickly closed the shop and made her way to Alhaja Amina's house. On the way, she noticed people standing in groups talking, but paid them no attention.

She ran straight into the living room of Alhaja Amina. Her friend was sitting on the floor, her eyes staring straight ahead at something fixed in the distance. It was as if she hadn't realised that I had stepped in.

Chinenye didn't like this at all.

She shook her hard. "What is it? Why are you like this?"

Alhaja Amina didn't even turn to look at her as she spoke. "I told you the Jade would be the death of us. My husband is a murderer. He has killed them all," she whispered, tears streaming down her cheeks.

"What?" Chinenye screamed.

After Alhaja Amina finished narrating all that had transpired at the farm, a cold fear swept through Chinenye's entire body. Her body had gone numb, thoughts disoriented, teeth clattered, imagination filled with so much horror that when the enormity of the situation finally hit her, she scrambled to let her thoughts out. "You can't stay here, Alhaja. You have to run away. They may come looking for him here. Who knows what they will do to you?"

"No, Chinenye! This is my home. I won't run away."

Chinenye burst into tears then. *How could the situation have come to this?* They both cried. They sat together until darkness descended.

"You have to go home, my friend. Your family needs you," Alhaja Amina said.

"No, I can't leave you."

"You have to go," Alhaja Amina stated firmly. "Go!"

Chinenye cried all the way home. She nursed a fear deep inside that she would never see her friend again.

The next day she couldn't go to the shop. Her husband stopped her from leaving the house because he didn't want her to go visit Alhaja Amina. He didn't think it was safe. Nobody knew what would happen. The situation was very tense all around Doka. The fact that the police had been compromised left a sour taste in everyone's mouth.

***

In the basement, the Military Colonel was trying very hard to keep his cool. "I can't believe what has just happened."

"Why? Isn't that what you were trying to do as well?" the lecturer questioned him with a snort of derision.

"I know!" the Military Colonel said. "But not to wipe out the entire family. All the sons are dead except for Mustapha, and that is because he wasn't there. I was going to teach them a lesson, but never did it cross my mind to do something so despicable."

"The late Alhaji Suleiman must be writhing in pain and agony in his grave. He was a peacemaker; one of the pillars of Doka and Kaduna in general. He shouldn't have been paid back this way. Alhaji Ali has committed a great crime," the minister added, sorrowfully.

"The deed has been done! Shouldn't we be moving forward? The opposition is gone," the businessman said with a straightforward approach.

"How can you even say this so soon? The dead haven't even been buried yet. Have some decency!" the minister shouted.

The lecturer inspected them one after the other. He had received information that he had turned a blind eye to. He had considered it false and placed it in a box never to be opened. It was difficult to contemplate the fact that such was true. But judging from what was playing out before him; the information wasn't far from the truth. He needed to look into it.

***

Loud wails rented the air as the women wept uncontrollably, rolling on the ground. They were cries of deep sorrow and sadness. Even the little ones cried, too. The dead bodies had been moved into the compound. Twenty-four sons and fifty grandsons had been killed; with only ten surviving grandsons left. They had died defending their own. Mustapha was too gutted and broken to weep.

He had failed.

He had failed his father.

He had failed them all.

CHAPTER TWENTY-ONE

Alhaja Amina sat cross-legged in her living room, faithfully watching the entrance. She had refused to take her bath and eat a meal. Earlier in the day, she had asked her helpers to take their leave.

Only one of them had stubbornly refused to do so. She was right now seated beside her madam. When her back ached from sitting up for too long, she lay down on the floor, and in a couple of ticks, slept off.

She woke up later to the sound of voices. She opened her eyes to darkness. The little illumination in the room came from the moonlight streaming in through the open window. It didn't leave much to see though. She must have slept off for too long, and her madam hadn't bothered to light a candle. She could only make out the outline of their bodies because she knew them well. The voices belonged to her Master, Alhaji Ali, who stood at the centre of the living room, and his wife. She doubted if he was aware that she was there.

"No!" Alhaja Amina said firmly. "I won't leave with a murderer."

Alhaji Ali grabbed her arms. "Don't you ever call me that again," he snapped. "I did this for us so we can have a better life. Go and grab a few things, and let's leave."

"Leave to where?" Alhaja Amina hissed. "Don't try to pull me into your dastardly act. You did it because of your greed. Where do you want to escape to? Don't you know that wherever you run to, your sins will find you?"

Alhaji Ali had reached the tail end of his patience. "You stupid woman! I could have left without coming back for you. But I made a sacrifice to come back, yet you give me this attitude. Stop being unreasonable and go get your things. We haven't got time to waste."

Alhaja Amina cackled like a deranged woman. Her husband tried to shut her mouth and they began struggling. Their scuffle masked the entrance of two men, who stealthily walked in.

The help's gaze was on the ensuing scuffle as she contemplated what to do. Hence, she didn't notice their entrance either.

It happened fast. They were over the head of Alhaji Ali in a flash.

Alhaja Amina hadn't even summoned the words to raise the alarm before she heard the gasp of surprise from her husband as he was struck from behind; the bag he held onto fell to the ground. She welcomed death as the machete descended on her neck. She fell to the floor, gasping for breath as blood gushed out of her wound.

One of the men spat on the prone body of Alhaji Ali. "You killed my father. A life for a life!"

They left without seeing the helper cowering in a dark corner; neither did they see the bag on the floor.

The helper rushed to her madam, bawling as she watched life slip away from Alhaja Amina. Another intruder walked in, and the helper sprang up in alarm. They had returned. How would she defend herself?

"What is happening here?" a female voice called out. "Why is it so dark?"

It wasn't them. The helper's voice quavered as she asked, "Who are you?"

Just then, the lady saw the bodies on the floor. She fell to her knees and cradled the bodies in her hands. "No!"

Alhaja Amina sputtered a faint breath.

"Mum, please hold on. Let me get help." Hadiza made to get up, but her mother held her firmly with the last ounce of strength she could muster. She was trying to say something through a mouthful of blood. Hadiza drew her ear closer to her mother's mouth. She listened attentively as her mother spoke before she took her last breath.

A heart-wrenching scream pierced through the silence of the darkness.

***

Neighbours woke up the next morning to the sight of the bodies of Alhaji Ali and his wife, neatly covered up in white sheets, carefully laid outside his house. Hadiza, the helper, and the bag had disappeared.

***

In one of the stalls at the market, a trader sold tomatoes. They were plump, red, and very attractive to look at. They were arranged on metal tins according to their sizes and prices. The trader was pleased with his tomatoes. He rubbed his hands excitedly in anticipation of the money they would fetch him that afternoon. He settled himself on a stool as he batted the flies away with a hand fan.

Nnamdi was on his way out of the market. He had purchased the items he needed to cook Egusi soup that afternoon. He whistled as he angled a path out of the market, his mind fixed on the soup he was going to cook for dinner with the large chunks of meat and dry fish he had purchased. It would be a nice way to end the day after the back-breaking work of lifting heavy bags of rice from Mallam Sule's truck. He would definitely have a good sleep after indulging himself in a good meal.

The tomato trader's stall was one of those he passed on his way out. He stopped in his tracks, staring at the tomatoes. He had seen a number of them in various stalls in the market; but this was different. It looked fresh and succulent. His mind quickly conjured an image of a plate of jollof rice laced with pieces of meat at the top. Nnamdi couldn't resist. He made his way to the stall.

"*Sannu*," he greeted.

"*Sannu Kadai*," the trader responded.

Nnamdi pointed at the tomatoes. "*Nawane?*"

The trader told him.

"Haba! Isn't it too much? *Nawane gaskiya?* Make me your customer, eh?"

The trader snorted in anger. "You are not my customer. If you can't buy it, go elsewhere."

Nnamdi didn't appreciate the tone of his voice. "What makes you think I can't buy it?" he huffed. "You don't have to be rude."

The trader rose to his feet. "What do you mean by being rude? This is my land! I will say whatever I please. If you can pay for it, why argue? You expect me to sell it less than I should, eh, greedy Igbo man. Please, leave my stall."

Nnamdi dropped his bag. "Did you call me greedy because I am Igbo? Is that why you want to sell the tomatoes at an outrageous price? Don't think you can control me because you people are the ruling government. Igbos would never be marginalised. I will stand in front of this stall for as long as I want."

That is how it started.

A shove.

A push.

A little scuffle.

Raised voices.

Blown out fight.

It was stroked by ethnic sentiments; coupled with the bitterness from the civil war and the North's wish to be divided due to the discovery of Jade. The flame burned all through the market. As a flame ignites, spreads, and turns into a huge fire; so did it escalate and spread beyond the market, and into the heart of Doka.

**

Chinenye was in her house with little Ngozi, wondering how she could send a message across to Alhaja Amina, when Chijioke rushed in.

"We have to run. The Igbos and Hausas are fighting."

She was trying to wrap her mind around what he said when Yakubu broke inside. He was the son of late Alhaji Danladi whom Chijioke's father had worked for, and in whose compound they lived.

"Come with me into my house. We will protect you," he promised.

They ran into his house and were kept safe while the fighting raged on. At the end of the day, casualties littered the streets with dead bodies strewn about from both tribes. Chinenye wasn't faring better either, as she had received news of the death of her friend, Alhaja Amina. The news shocked her to the bone,and she retreated to a corner to mourn the loss of her friend.

Chijioke tried to comfort her, but he met with resistance. Before he left to allow her some privacy, he whispered in her ears: "It's time we leave and return to the East. My parents are gone. We will start a new life there."

Later that evening, Chinenye was still seated by the corner, clothed with a garment of deep sorrow as she spoon-fed Ngozi, when Yakubu's wife came to inform me that she had a visitor. She wondered who it was.

A woman dressed in a burka—a one piece veil that covers the face and body leaving just a mesh screen to see through- approached her. "*Sannu.*"

"*Sannu dazuwa,*" she replied.

She urged her to sit down. "Please, who are you?"

"I am Hadiza Muhammed, the daughter of Alhaja Amina Muhammed."

Chinenye rose in shock. She could hardly dare to breathe. Hadiza was here in the flesh. *What could this possibly mean? Did this have something to do with the death of her parents?* Hadiza took the questions right out of her mouth.

She drew closer to her. Her voice sounded thin and hoarse from weeping. "My mother sent me to you. She passed a message to me as I held her in my arms before she took her last breath." Her voice cracked. She paused for a bit before she continued: "You have to promise me that what I tell you will remain between us."

Chinenye didn't know what to say. She barely managed to nod in acknowledgement. Silent tears leaked out of her eyes as Hadiza narrated what she had seen when she arrived.

She brought out what looked like a small stone and handed it to her. "My mother asked me to give this to you."

It took some time before Chinenye could find the words to speak. "What will you do now?"

"I have to leave immediately. I covered up from my head to my toes so no one would recognise me. I couldn't even give my parents a decent burial. I'm sure they understand. It's not safe here."

"I understand," Chinenye said as she drew her in for a hug. Hadiza held on tightly to her as she surrendered to her emotions. When she had gotten control of herself, Chinenye continued: "You can return to Lagos and even marry your boyfriend, the Igbo boy. You will be happy."

Hadiza's back straightened. "I will return to Lagos, and from there, move back to London. My fears have been confirmed. Can you see what has taken place?" she asked, waving her hands in the air. "The bloodshed? All for what?" she lamented, her voice rising. "We can't get married. This is the end."

Hadiza got up and walked away, leaving Chinenye to mourn the loss of her friend. The gift of the Jade was no comfort to her. Her friend was gone. She was right. It was the death of them! The death of her friend and her husband; the death of their friendship; the death of Hadiza's trust in humanity. She worried about her, but she was beyond her reach. There was nothing left here. Indeed, it was time to leave.

***

Mustapha was a shadow of his former self. He had failed. He was no leader. His father and brothers were gone. What gave him the right to live? Was he better than them? What he was contemplating was a taboo. In fact, it was an open doorway to hell.

Allah would never forgive him.

But he couldn't live with himself anymore. How could he wake up every morning to a compound empty of their presence and voices? He would save himself from further torture. He knew what to do. All he needed was a rope.

***

In Grandma's room, tears streamed down their cheeks. Gregory's heart was heavy. Pain was evident on their faces. This was what grandma had referred to when she informed them at the beginning of the story that some parts would make them cry. This was what Gregory had longed to hear: the personal stories. But now they left him empty, shaken, and hollow-eyed.

CHAPTER TWENTY-TWO

The air was thick with the thoughts of the traditional rulers. They held the traditional form of authority in the country. The Sultan of Sokoto was the spiritual leader of all Muslims. The Emir of Kano was second to him. They were in a meeting at the palace of the Sultan of Sokoto.

The palace was built in 1808. It was the oldest and largest traditional palace, situated on about thirty-three acres of land; built on open plains and surrounded by walls up to fifteen feet high.

The Emir of Kano, clothed in a royal robe and a turban, started off the conversation. "The violence has spread. There have been pockets of fighting reported all over the country."

"It has to stop!" the Sultan, also dressed in traditional royal regalia with a turban to match, blurted out. "The civil war began with the death of my predecessor, Sir Ahmadu Bello. The hatred, bitterness, and divisive spirit has to be dealt with."

"If we don't do something fast, we would be plunged into another civil war. Precious lives have been lost. We can't afford any more losses, be it human or otherwise," the Emir said.

"Let's send messages across to our fellow counterparts immediately. We must not allow our country to disintegrate further. We are bigger than the political structure. We must take a decisive action," said the Sultan.

***

"Mum, something is wrong," Clement said as he barged into his mother's quarters.

"Of course, my son! The entire country is in an uproar. I had believed that the bloodshed had ended with the end of the war," she said, saddened. "I have to finish up what I am doing. All the traditional rulers have been summoned to a meeting in Lagos. Your father leaves first thing tomorrow morning. Lagos was chosen because it is a neutral place."

Clement hadn't known that. He had been cocooned in his world. But that wasn't why he was here. "Mum, you aren't even paying me attention."

Lolo Chizoba took a proper look at her son. She observed his sunken eyes and cheeks, and general disheveled look. It alarmed her. "What is it, my son?"

"It's Hadiza!" he cried out. "I can't get in touch with her. She was supposed to call me, but she hasn't. I'm afraid, Mum. Was she killed alongside her parents?"

The fighting had certainly found its way to the palace. Her son looked crushed. Lolo Chizoba had no words to console him. The look of anguish on his face tore through her. She enveloped him in an embrace as they both cried—he for losing the love of his life, she for the unnecessary deaths and mindless killing. *Was it worth it?*

***

The look on the military colonel's face was murderous. His face was a mirror of his feelings. "What is this I am hearing?" he asked the entire room filled with his fellow members of the Kaduna Mafia. "What are the traditional rulers trying to do?"

"I'm just as confused as you are. This puts a stop to our plans," said the lecturer.

"If they try to unite the country, then we will lose our domination of the Jade. Can't they see that?" the bank manager asked.

"This is beyond us. There is nothing we can do," the cabinet minister said in resignation.

There was a knock at the door. That had never happened before. The hotel owner got up and opened the door. He spoke in a hushed voice to whoever was on the other side of the door before he shut the door and grabbed a remote control. "The president is giving a speech."

They all watched the face on the screen as he reeled out his ten minutes speech. When he was through, there was complete silence. The military colonel struggled to breathe. The lecturer feared he might suffer a heart attack.

The bank manager broke the silence, mimicking the tone of the president. "What's this with his motto: unity and faith, peace and progress?"

"So the mineral resources are for the good of the entire country now?" the minister added. "What hogwash!"

"I am sure you are happy now, are you not?" the lecturer said.

"What are you talking about? Who are you referring to?" the hotel owner asked.

"It's you I am referring to." The lecturer pointed to the businessman. "I saw you smiling during the speech. There's no need to hide. Your schemes are out in the open, traitor."

"What are you saying?" The business man leaped to his feet.

"I received reports from one of my students. I couldn't believe it at first; that you were in talks with a rich easterner that would see you both enjoy the benefits of the Oil and the Jade through the merging of your businesses. You were ready to give our Jade away. But your reaction has given you away. You are not as smart as you think you are."

"No, you are wrong! Let me…"

A gunshot echoed in the room, cutting his words off.

The businessman slumped on the chair, staring wide-eyed at the ceiling, a hole on his forehead.

Whatever he wanted to say, it dissolved into the blood that trickled down to his face.

The others stared in shock while the military colonel strutted away.

***

In the palace of the Oba of Lagos, a meeting the likes of which had never taken place was in motion. In attendance were the: Obi of Onitsha, Sultan of Sokoto, Emir of Kano, Oni of Ife, Alaafin of Oyo, Dein of Agbor, Oba of Benin, Olu of Itsekiri, Olubadan of Ibadan, and the host—the Oba of Lagos.

The meeting should have put media houses in a frenzy as they scrambled to get the attention of the royals, or the paparazzi photographers taking pictures of the beautiful costumes and display of royalty imbued in their gait and demeanour, but it wasn't a time to show off. They were all here to fulfill their mandates as the traditional rulers of their people. The media was only allowed to be present in order to convey their message at the end of the meeting.

The Oba of Lagos opened the floor: "I welcome you all to my palace. I would have loved to entertain immediately, as it's obligatory fora host. There would be time for that later. We are here for something greater. Our beloved country, Nigeria, is on the verge of an imminent collapse."

"It would only collapse if we allow it," the Emir of Kano pointed out.

"We are here to put an end to it. We must come up with a solution," added the Oba of Benin.

"The traditional form of authority has been in existence from the pre-colonial times and has survived till today. We owe this country our best," the Olubadan of Ibadan said.

"But how can all this be happening?" the Obi of Onitsha questioned. "There is no love amongst us."

"And we are being exploited and dominated forcefully! Is that rulership? Is that democracy?" the Dein of Agbor asked.

"God has blessed us with mineral resources to enrich us and make our lives better. But how have we utilised it? We have abused the opportunity," the Alaafin of Oyo said.

"The mineral resources are for the benefit of everyone and not just for a certain group or tribe," the Sultan of Sokoto asserted.

"The exploitation has to be stopped alongside the senseless killing and fighting. We have to prove to the world that we can take care of our affairs. That we can live together as one!" the Oni of Ife's voice boomed out.

"First, we need to make a public appearance to show our people that the traditional institutions are united and believe in the same course. This would go a long way to show them that they need to embrace peace and unity. We are one; irrespective of tribe or religion," the Olu of Itsekiri clarified.

"And then we must pay a visit to the Officeof the President. All the mineral resources must be put to the use of the people. We call for an end to exploitation and disintegration. Do we all agree?" the Oba of Lagos asked.

"Yes!" they all chorused in a loud voice; their voices resonating beyond the palace walls.

***

Some weeks later, Chinenye had just finished feeding Ngozi and lay down to rest. The journey back to the East fared worse than the initial trip to Kaduna several years ago. She was happy to be back home; most especially about something else, as she caressed her stomach lightly. She had just found out she was a few weeks pregnant. She recalled how she had rejoiced over her first pregnancy with her late friend Alhaja Amina. She quickly wiped her tears away as she heard the footsteps of her husband entering the house.

While he took his bath, she picked up the newspaper he had returned with to peruse its contents. The front page had the picture of the president and all the traditional rulers. She had heard of the meeting on radio and the promises from the president to use his tenure to ensure the promulgation of laws that ensured the equitable distribution of resources. She was aware that people were reluctant to believe him. They called it the 'Politician's Story'. But she believed it. The traditional rulers were the heroes of the day. They had taken a stand together; a greater message than even the speech and promises of the president.

She noticed a short story bulletin at the bottom of the page. A military colonel suspected to be a member of the Kaduna Mafia had suffered a heart attack and died that morning. *What a pity,* she thought, as she dropped the paper to attend to her husband.

***

Clement Okoye walked the entire length of the beach. He wouldn't give up. He would keep coming back until the day his Hadiza would return to him. His love for her would never die.

***

The president was in a close meeting with his chief of staff and heads of security parastatals. They had been in talks for two hours. It was time to round off the meeting.

"It is quite unfortunate that the people at the heart of this are dead; but it is to our advantage. The betrayals and greed have died with them. The political atmosphere is very tense and the accord is still fragile. It must be protected. The general public doesn't need to know the nitty-gritty of what happened. Let's keep it under wraps. It's for the good of everyone."

.

CHAPTER TWENTY-THREE

Six months later.

Gregory had returned to his former self. The school session had ended for the year. They were on a long-term break. Thankfully, he had come out with good grades. After the story about Jade had been completed, his cognitive ability was restored and he could face his studies again.

Also, his friends had welcomed him back warmly. They teased him non-stop about his brief hiatus. They were such cool friends. Another great piece of news was that Chima finally won the heart of Adaeze. So funny, wasn't it? Musa clearly didn't stand a chance against Chima's antics. They were now a group of six with two females. During the lunch break, Adaeze supplied them with enough doughnuts—an added perk of her friendship. They were the envy of all.

As for Grandma, her situation got worse. She had entered stage five. Though painful, there was nothing they could do except to take care of her. Before she got worse though, she did something that still gave Gregory goose bumps whenever he thought about it. Grandma called Gregory and his parents into her room. There, she presented the Jade to Gregory. She said it was his. He deserved to have it. Gregory's mum shed a few tears. It was as if Grandma was passing her story onto Gregory. In fact, Gregory had nicknamed the Jade 'a memory stone'. It had locked in it memories of both good and bad.

Gregory didn't know what to do with it. The price it fetched stunned him. His father was in possession of it until such a time he would need it. Then, he would be mature enough to make a wise decision.

As for Mr Julius, he became a different man. He had been a part of a huge discovery. There were discussions between him and Gregory's parents. Talks about writing a biography about the life history of Grandma. They all agreed that the story needed to be told. He was now a man on a different mission. He was writing the biography as he looked into publishing options. No doubt, the manuscript would be scooped up by major publishing houses. It was too juicy to be ignored.

Sometimes, Gregory wondered about Hadiza and the bag filled with Jade stones that she had disappeared with. Wherever she was, she must be a very wealthy woman. He hoped she found peace and happiness.

As for Clement Okoye, Gregory pictured a man weather-beaten, emotionally worn-thin, yet still hopelessly searching for the love of his life as he patrolled the beach. May his wish be granted, he hoped!

That was the power of Jade. It sunk its teeth into you and left trickles of its power that never faded away. They were all its subjects.

THE END

About the Author

Tracey Chizoba Fletcher

Amb. Dr Tracey Chizoba Fletcher is a five-time published author who loves to draw attention to the beauty of Africa through her writings.

She is a book editor and publishing consultant, and the CEO/Founder of Zoba's Facilities.

When she isn't immersed in writing or editing, she uses her time and resources to push for the causes she believes in.